HER RELUCTANT CHRISTMAS COWBOY STAR

THE CHRISTMAS STAR COLLECTION BOOK TWO

EDITH MACKENZIE

THE SMALL PUBLISHING HOUSE

Her Reluctant Christmas Cowboy Star (Cowboy Christmas, The Christmas Star Collection Book #2):

Images © DepositPhotos – pikselstock & Kotenko. Cover Design © Designed with Grace

❀ Created with Vellum

For everyone that needs a hug on Christmas. You're special

THREE MONTHS TILL CHRISTMAS

*S*uzie stared at the email. *The tenth anniversary of Luciano and Frankie's movie.* It couldn't be that long, could it? Gosh, she'd only been starting out in the business back then, barely twenty years old and filled with the naivety of youth. Luciano and Frankie were so in love and now had children who were starting out in junior rodeos for themselves. Ash and Kirk Cooper had gone on to become Hollywood royalty and one of the most powerful couples in the industry. Savannah was now just about the most famous barrel racer in history, and Bryce followed her around like a lovesick puppy.

Suzie sighed. She would be coming off a three-month movie shoot in Nairobi and had hoped to go down to Veronica's ranch for at least a fleeting visit before she had to do a few quick shoots her agent had scheduled in. Still, it had been years since they'd all been in the same room together— probably at the wrap party for the film. And it wasn't like she wouldn't see Veronica. She'd be going to the ranch for Christmas anyway. And dang if it wouldn't be all sorts of fun to go to the reunion. There were so many good memories.

Especially that shy young cowboy who had come in as one of the extras so many years ago. He'd been all sorts of cute, even if he'd never quite managed to do more than smile at her. What was his name again? Greyson.

Yes, indeed. Greyson was definitely one of those good memories.

TWO MONTHS BEFORE CHRISTMAS

The dress was cute—button up with a matching red Peter Pan collar and thin leather belt that encircled her narrow waist. The umbrella print added just enough character to make the dress a little quirky, which was more than fine in Suzie's book.

Now, what shoes? The goth black platform boots? *Maybe a little too theatrical.* Strappy heels? *Boring.* Her eyes lit up when she spied the perfect pair of red sequin-covered ballet shoes, complete with matching red ribbons to tie around her ankles. Slipping her feet into the shoes, she tried to envisage what Greyson would look like now. He'd had such a baby face back then, all big gooey brown eyes that you just wanted to melt into. Ten years was a long time. He was bound to look older now. She stood peering into the mirror as she made final adjustments. If this outfit didn't knock his socks off, then he wasn't ready for Suzie Bellamy.

Clutching her fairy floss martini later at the reunion, it was becoming quite clear that she hadn't needed to worry about what he thought about her outfit. Peering around, she hadn't been able to catch sight of him yet.

"Can you see Harper?" Luciano, the famous Brazilian bull rider who the film had been made about asked his wife. The willowy blonde rolled her eyes at him. "She's fine, Luc," Frankie said, an Australian accent still shading her words even after a decade of living in Texas.

Frankie and a few of her Australian friends, Deb, Megan and Chloe, had all moved to the States to chase their dreams all those years ago and ended up finding love as well. For someone who worked in the movie industry, Suzie wasn't surprised they'd made a movie out of Luciano and Frankie's story. Honestly, she'd felt privileged to be able to work with them when she did. And let's face it. If she'd never worked that movie, she never would have met that handsome young cowboy who she was still yet to sight.

"Junior," Luciano said to the strapping young man beside him. Goodness, at ten years old, it wasn't long before he would be a teenager. It was shocking to think that, when she'd first met Luciano and Frankie, the twins had only just started growing in their mother's belly. "Go find your sister and make sure she's staying out of trouble."

"Gracie and Teeny are with them. I'm sure it's fine," Deb reassured him. "You let them babysit all the time."

"I almost didn't let Teeny out the house this evening," Teeny's father, Travis, said to the man beside him. "You should have seen what she wanted to wear."

"Gracie's not too bad yet," Deb's husband, Mitch, replied, taking a sip of his beer. "She's still happy in jeans and boots and hanging around the horses."

"Leave Teeny alone. She's fourteen," Travis's wife, Chloe, said firmly.

"And they're good girls," added Frankie.

Suzie took another sip of her cocktail before excusing herself. Maybe it was time to work the room. She was never going to find Greyson if she stayed in one spot.

~

THE EDGE of the cardboard was sharp against his skin as he rubbed his thumb against the invitation in his pocket. *The reunion.* Ten years felt like a lifetime ago. Maybe he was being stupid by going. *But maybe she would be there.* He pulled down the leg of his jeans—the best he owned—where it had ridden up over his boots. The leather of his boots was worn, but he'd cleaned them up the best he could.

"Is that what you're wearing?" Bronson sneered from the doorway. His stepbrother's outfit was one he hadn't seen before, which didn't surprise him since he was always spending money on clothes. "Rob, come check out this clown."

His other stepbrother looked him slowly up and down, derision stamped across his plumb features. "It looks like you raided a Goodwill dumpster."

"I got these last Christmas." He didn't need to add that he'd saved up and purchased them for himself and that he'd been carefully keeping the shirt for just the right special occasion. The ranch was doing it tough since his dad died and left his stepmother in charge. Even though he'd worked every day, he'd only taken enough of a wage to cover his fuel and a few miscellaneous things in over year. Not that it seemed to help the state of the ranch at all. The barn had a serious lean that gravity would soon win, and the house was in sore need of a new roof. Not to mention the tractor that was only running thanks to his ingenuity and a lot of prayer. None of that seemed to worry his stepbrothers. They always seemed to have the best of everything.

"I've got work clothes better than that." Rob elbowed his brother in the ribs.

"I've clean thrown out clothes like that," countered Bronson. Chuckling, the brothers gave him one last mocking glance before heading down the stairs.

Greyson quickly smoothed his hair down before grabbing his hat off the dresser. It had been one of the last things his dad had given him. Settling it in place, he hurried down after the others. Reaching the front door, his hand froze as he heard the revving of an engine before it roared down the driveway. Why did he ever assume that, just because they were all going to the same place, they'd give him a lift in one of their big, fancy trucks? Maybe because it *would have* saved him on a little fuel. *Or m*aybe because they were supposed to be family. Sighing, he turned the doorknob and headed outside, making his way to where his old beaten-up truck was parked. She might not be fancy, but she was reliable—at least, when she wasn't breaking down. The door screeched in protest as he opened it, and a bellow from the field behind the barn made him pause. It didn't sound like the normal calls the cattle made. It wasn't fearful like a coyote was bothering them, but still, he'd better check it out. Closing the door, he set forth to investigate.

Rounding the corner, he saw a cow in the distance, lying on the ground. She looked to be struggling to deliver her calf. Long strides ate up the ground until he was by her, her distended sides heaving as her eyes rolled wildly. "Easy, girl." He soothed the cow as he unbuttoned the cuff of his shirt and began to roll his sleeves up. "I'm here, and I ain't going nowhere till we get you sorted."

WHERE WAS HE? *Maybe he didn't get an invite.* Suzie shook her head. That was silly. Everyone got one. In the distance, she could see Sra Ana and Senhor Eduardo deep in conversation with the caterer for the film. When they'd been shooting, Sra

Ana had become somewhat of an honorary grandmother for the set. The little Brazilian lady's husband, Senhor Eduardo, had also been a regular visitor as he'd watched the film about one of his protégés take place. *Maybe he'd gotten married and wasn't interested in coming.* It was a crushing thought that left Suzie disquieted. Somehow she hadn't considered that he might not be single when she saw him again. He was most definitely single whenever she thought about him. Her eyes widened in alarm. *Maybe he was dead.*

THE GROUND WAS slick with birth fluid. The calf, now safely delivered, rested beside his exhausted mother, the cow's tongue already setting to work to clean her baby. Both seemed to be doing well despite Greyson having to help pull the calf free. Greyson looked down at his watch. The reunion had already started, but there was still time if he hurried to get there before it was over. *To see her.* He glanced down in dismay at his once new clothes now covered in muck and the products of labor. Maybe a quick shower first, and then a change into the cleanest of his work clothes. Rubbing his hands on his damp and slimy jeans, he briskly headed back to the house. No time to waste.

THE GORGEOUS AUBURN-HAIRED woman clad in a white pant suit stroked the arm of the man beside her as she animatedly talked to a strikingly similar woman clad in a flowing boho dress cinched in at the waist. Suzie had worked with Ash on her last film, but hadn't seen her twin sister, Savannah—now a world champion barrel racer several times over—since the filming on Frankie and Luciano's movie had ended.

"You should see him, Ash. Gabi started doing embryo transfers from Nova a couple of years ago, and Mercury is from the first foal crop that's now ready to start breaking in. It's like he already knows how to run the pattern. Frankie and Chloe say they've never seen a horse go the way he does, and they rode Sampson and Delila." Savannah gazed up at her husband, Bryce, for confirmation. "Isn't that right?"

"Sure is," he readily agreed.

"You should come out and see him and, if you haven't forgotten how to, have a ride," Savannah cheekily said to her twin.

"It's not like I don't come out between films to visit. I ride then, if you haven't forgotten." Ash narrowed her eyes at her sister. "Anyway, I was always the better rider, so even if I'm a bit rusty, it's still better than what the poor horse has been putting up with."

Suzie wasn't sure what Kirk, Ash's movie star husband, said to try to defuse the situation. You'd think by now that he'd be used to the way those two constantly bickered. It was actually one of her fondest memories of filming. The sisters had certainly been entertaining. Sipping her cocktail, she returned to scanning the room. *It's official. He isn't coming.* It was hard to ignore the cold weight that settled in her belly. *It's not like he was that cute anyway.*

Then a movement near the entrance, slow and uncertain, caught her attention. *Could it be?* He was just as broad-shouldered as she remembered, casting his gaze almost fretfully around as if lost. Not bothering to give her excuses—the conversation had already moved on anyway—Suzie squeezed through people until she was by his side. Taking a deep breath, the moment feeling somewhat surreal now that it had arrived, she smiled up at him.

"Hi."

He looked jittery, like a colt ready for flight. Geeze, she

needed to stop listening to all these cowboy and cowgirls. His velvety brown eyes were as soft and gentle as she remembered, if a little more tired and careworn.

"I'm not sure if you remember me. I'm Suzie. I was the makeup artist on set, but I mainly saw you around the catering tent when you were on break."

"I remember you." His voice was slow as molasses on a cold morning. Delicious shivers danced through her, erupting in goosebumps at the sound. "Your hair is different now."

Surprised, she touched her pale lavender-colored hair. "Probably. I can't remember what it was back then. I'm always changing it."

"It was longer and blue." Those puppy dog eyes flicked over her pixie cut. "It looks nice."

Suzie found herself momentarily lost for words. He remembered what her hair was like. Rushing to fill the silence, she said the first thing that sprung to mind. "I love your hat."

The look he sent her way warmed her all the way down to her toes. Without breaking the smoldering eye contact, he reached up and removed it from his head, hesitated a moment, and set it gently down on hers. "It looks good on you."

"Hank—that's Veronica's fiancé—says that for the amount of time I spend on their ranch, I should get myself a hat. I mean, I do like accessories. Is it okay to think of a cowboy hat as an accessory? Hank seems to put a lot of importance on his hat, so maybe it's more like a badge. Like a rancher badge?" *Oh gosh, that sounds stupid. Think of something to change the topic.* "That's where I'm actually spending Christmas. Maybe I should ask Santa for one." Why was she babbling about Christmas?

In desperation, she took a gulp of her cocktail to silence

the stream of words flooding from her mouth. Daring to look up at him, she was relieved to see an easy smile on his lips, his attention focused on her. *He really is a good listener.*

～

It was going well! The girl Greyson hadn't been able to stop thinking about—the one he'd crushed on since he'd seen her like a rainbow amongst the gray clouds on the movie set— remembered him. Man, he'd been so shy. Not much had changed. The entire time he'd been an extra, he'd tried to pluck up the courage to say more than a simple hello or smile. But every time he'd found himself lost in the captivating way her eyes sparkled with pure life, all words would flee his mind. He was pretty much convinced she'd thought he was a simpleton. And now she was wearing his hat. Sure, she might not understand what it meant when a cowboy gave a girl his hat to wear, but she—she was wearing it!

"I didn't think you were going to show up. I mean, the night is nearly half over."

Had she been waiting for him? Greyson swallowed, looking to see if a waiter was near to snatch a glass of anything to quench his suddenly dry mouth. "Something came up at the ranch."

Relief flooded her dancing eyes, her lush lips breaking into a smile. "Oh, well, I hope it wasn't anything too serious. At least you're here now. That's all that matters."

Greyson finally managed to snag a bottle of beer from a passing attendant, catching the gaze of one of his step- brothers in the distance. *Let them stare. He* was talking to a beautiful woman, *after all.*

"Look at me, I haven't even let you get a drink before I'm all over you." *All over you.* Now that was an exciting thought.

Suzie gave a breathless giggle. "I need to go powder my nose, but maybe we can keep talking when I get back?"

She said it like it was a question. Where did she think he would go? He was exactly where he wanted to be. Talking to her. "I'd like that."

Suzie bestowed on him a beaming smile that had him returning it before he could even think about it. Greyson watched as she slipped between people, disappearing to the other side of the room. It was like one of his dreams. The ones where Suzie had come to life.

"Look who thinks he's all that," Rob sneered from behind him.

Poof. Just like that, all the happiness evaporated. His shoulders drooping, he turned around to face his tormentors.

Bronson broke out in laughter. "What are you wearing? I mean, the other outfit wasn't exactly primo, but this is just pathetic."

"Heck, I'd be embarrassed to be seen in that." Rob wrinkled his nose. "I mean, look at you."

"I wouldn't even clean out the pig pen in it," Bronson agreed. "But you seem right at home in the filth. Maybe you should go back home and wallow in it. It's where you belong. Quick, before anyone sees you here with your betters."

Greyson could feel the burn of shame sweep across his face. Is this what Suzie thought? Had she only been nice to him because she'd felt sorry for him? Feeling stupid, a shudder of humiliation set his feet into motion. Without risking another glance at his stepbrothers, he fled into the night.

SIX WEEKS TILL CHRISTMAS

"*I* can't wait to finish up the last of my commitments for the year. I'm so ready for the holiday season." Veronica's voice was tired on the other end of the line. She was in the final stages of shooting a film in Nairobi. "I miss Hank and Lulu whenever I'm away, but this time of the year, it's worse. I can't believe it's only been a year since we met. I can't imagine life without them now."

Without my family. That's what she'd meant to say, Suzie was sure of it. And she couldn't blame her. Hank and Lulu were awesome. Lucky for Suzie, she was considered part of that elite group. Her gaze drifted across to where Greyson's black Stetson sat pride of place between her hair products and makeup on her dresser. *Why had he left like that?* Everything had been going so well. At least, she'd thought so, until her bladder had ruined the moment. When she'd returned, he'd been nowhere to be found. *If he didn't want to talk to me, he could have just said so. No need to run off into the night like a coward.* A forlorn sigh escaped her.

"Why don't you just track down your cowboy and be done with it?" Laughing exasperation sounded in Suzie's ear.

She jerked her eyes guiltily away from the hat. "Who says I'm thinking about Greyson?"

"Let me count the ways. First, the sigh. I've heard less melodramatic sounds in an amateur Romeo and Juliet." Suzie could just imagine her friend in her hotel suite, phone held between her ear and shoulder to free up her hands to tick off each item. She smiled. She really did have the best friend. "Second, I'm pretty sure you haven't listened to a thing I've said."

"That's not true. You were talking about missing Hank and Lulu," Suzie protested. *That was what she'd been talking about, right?*

"And what did I say after that?"

There'd been more? "Um…"

"That's my point. Just call him already."

"I don't even have his number," Suzie protested weakly.

"Oh, please. As if that's ever stopped you before. Suzie, you're a true force of nature, and it's one of the things I love about you. It's fine to be all damsel in the tower waiting to be rescued by Prince Charming. I get it, I really do. But that's not you, so snap out of it." Suzie could feel the energy in her friend's voice as she warmed to her topic. "Get onto the organizers of the reunion. Obviously, they know how to get in touch with him. He was there, wasn't he?" Not waiting for an answer, Veronica ploughed on. "Better still, give Ash a call. She should be able to give the best contact for that."

Again, she looked to the hat, thinking about the shyly smiling cowboy who had been wearing it. "I do have his hat. I really should return it to him."

"It's the least you can do."

FIVE WEEKS TILL CHRISTMAS

*T*he pitted metal was rough against Greyson's skin as he rested his forehead under the open hood of his truck. He'd been working like a dog on the ranch, stretching the stock feed as much as he could thanks to the pitiful amount of money his stepbrothers left in the account, and now his truck had decided to die on him. Despair sucked the hope from his soul. Surely there was more to life than endless hard work and struggle. When was it his chance for a little happiness?

A vision of his mother popped into his mind, radiant as she smiled at him on the porch swing, the sun making her hair glow. Loss buffeted him as he closed his eyes against the sting of tears. It wasn't meant to be like this. And Dad sure as heck shouldn't have married Irene and burdened him with Bronson and Rob. Greyson was almost convinced that Dad had just given up on life when he'd realized the mistake he'd made. The betrayal of him leaving the family ranch to his stepmom still hurt.

Thinking of things that couldn't be changed didn't help anyone. Pushing himself off his truck, he headed over to where crates containing parts he'd scavenged from wrecks were neatly stacked. Greyson prayed the part he needed was still here as he fossicked through the bits and pieces.

To make matters worse, his new hat still wasn't broken in the way he liked it. It sat too stiffly, the shape not quite right. Visions of his old hat sitting proudly atop Suzie's gorgeous lavender hair did take some of the sting out of it. The way her beautiful eyes had glowed up at him when he'd placed it on her … well, it filled him with all sorts of possessiveness, something that was, quite frankly, foreign to him. Especially when it came to women. Her in his hat had just felt right.

A dog barking outside drew his attention away from thinking of Suzie. *Bronson and Rob can't be back from town so soon. Usually they don't come home till all the bars are closed.* Curious when he heard the crunch of car tires on gravel, he went to the door of the barn. The clean electric car didn't look like it belong in these parts, and most certainly didn't belong to anyone he knew. The door opened, and a lavender head popped out, followed by the rest of her. *Suzie!* He gaped at her in silent disbelief.

"I'm so glad you're home. I hope I haven't come at a bad time?"

Befuddled, he continued to gawk at her until she nervously looked around. Embarrassment scalded his cheeks as he saw her take it all in. The wrecks of expensive toys his stepbrothers had brought home and ruined, leaving them to decay where they stood. The barn, almost comical in its dilapidated state. Defeated, he kicked at the rock beneath his feet. *Pathetic. That's what it looked like.* How did he tell her that it hadn't always been like this? The one saving grace was that Bronson and Rob weren't here to make it worse.

"Nope, this is as good as it gets."

Her eyes sparkled brighter than any person's eyes had a right to as she beamed at him. "Well then, I guess it's time I return this to you." Baffled, he watched her reach back inside the car before closing the door behind her. "I believe I have something that belongs to you." She held out his hat in front of her as proudly as one would display the Crown Jewels.

Greyson was beginning to wonder if he'd bumped his head when he was under his truck's hood. It was the only explanation for this surreal turn of events. "Thank you." Awkwardly, he made his way over to collect his hat. All the time, Suzie beamed at him. "How did you find me?" Not that he was complaining.

"Well, after you ran away at the reunion—what happened there, by the way? Was it me? Or did you get an emergency? Which I totally understand. Sometimes life gets in the way. I hope it wasn't me…" Suzie's hands danced in front of her, as lively as the stream of words flowing from her mouth. "My friend, Veronica, suggested that maybe I should return your hat to you. So, I called Ash—Ash Cooper, the girl who played Frankie?" She stopped to peer at him. He nodded when it was clear she required an answer. "She gave me the name of a contact for the company that organized the reunion. Turns out, she was on maternity leave. Then I had to wait for her replacement to get back to me and she wasn't really all over the reunion stuff, so then they tracked down the lady who was on leave and finally she got in contact with me. Turns out she had a beautiful baby boy." Suzie paused to smile happily to herself at the news. "And she gave me your address. So here I am." Doubt swirled behind her vivacious eyes. "Is it okay that I'm here?"

Okay? That was like asking if it was okay if the sun came up tomorrow. "I don't mind."

She reached out a hand to his. It was the lightest of touches and yet it felt like an earthquake had erupted beneath his feet. "I'm so relieved. I didn't want you to think I was some crazy stalker or, worse, that you really had run off to get away from me." Suzie's face scrunched up. "You didn't, did you?"

"No. As you said, something came up." *Think, brain. Think of something funny and witty that will keep her here talking.* "How long are you in town for?"

"Just the night." Her stomach gave a low rumble, setting her to giggling. Transfixed, Greyson didn't think he'd ever heard such a captivating sound as her laughter. "Excuse me. It's been a while since I ate."

"Do you have plans for dinner?" The words were out of his mouth before he could think. Maybe that was for the best. If he'd thought for too long, he was liable to keep them trapped in his head.

"I don't." Those lush lips curved into a coy smile. "Do you happen to know somewhere good to eat?"

"I do. And I reckon buying you dinner is the least I can do since you went to so much trouble to return my hat."

"I'd love to have dinner with you. And don't sweat it. I kinda enjoyed the journey of finding you." A delicate pink bloomed to life across her cheeks. "Is it best if I give you my number and you can text me the details of where you want to meet up?"

Quickly, he fumbled in his pocket, retrieved his phone, and handed it over to her. Suzie calmly tapped away before handing it back to him. "I need to finish up here and shower, but I won't keep you waiting too long." He grinned shyly at her when her belly rumbled again. "I don't want you starving."

Another giggle. Man, he could get used to it. "I'll head back to town and, I guess, see you soon."

Greyson watched as she got back into her little car and drove off, waving. As soon as she was out of sight, he let out a loud whoop. Then, remembering his truck wasn't running, he bolted back into the barn, praying that he could get it fixed and back to working order in record time. He was going to attempt it or die trying. It wasn't every day he had a date. Let alone one with a cute girl with a killer smile.

IT WAS FUNNY. Suzie had spent a couple of months in this part of Texas ten years ago when they'd been filming, but she'd never ventured to the small town that Greyson called home. She looked up the street again, hopeful for the lights of an approaching car. There wasn't much chance that she'd miss him since there was just the one rather forlorn main street. Settling back against the bench in front of what looked to have once been the bakery, she tried to imagine a young Greyson growing up here. The cracked sidewalk would have been smooth then. Obviously, the bakery would have been open for the young boy to purchase a fresh treat, maybe even some flowers in the old concrete planters. Now it just seemed to be shades of gray and depression.

The flash of lights glowing in the distance pulled her out of her doldrums. An alarming screeching noise sounded as it drew closer, forcing her to cover her ears with her hands for fear that she would be rendered deaf. Suzie stood frozen like a deer caught in the spotlight until it ground to a halt in front of her. Inside the dim interior of the cab, she could just make out a man wearing a cowboy hat. *Was it Greyson?*

Heart pounding beneath her cyan colored leather jacket, Suzie watched as Greyson slowly oozed from the car. "I'm sorry. Things took a little longer than I thought it would."

"That's okay." Suzie felt breathless. "It gave me time to admire the main street."

He looked up and down the street, taking in its sad state, and quirked a brow at her. "Really?"

"Okay, maybe it needs a little TLC. I was wondering where, exactly, you were planning on taking me to eat."

"There aren't exactly a lot of options here. There's the bar." Greyson pointed down the end of the street where loud music drifted from, a few trucks parked out front. "You take your own chances eating there. And then there's Ma's Diner, not be mistaken for any relation."

"I take it we're dining at Ma's then?"

"I don't feel like gambling with my health tonight. So, yes. Ma's." He gestured for her to precede him before falling into step beside her.

Suzie noticed that he placed himself between her and the traffic, not that there was much of it. Still, it was a thoughtful gesture, nonetheless. Something swelled in her chest that she couldn't quite place, but it felt good. Nice. She could get used to that feeling. It took her a moment to realize neither of them had spoken again. Now that he had answered her question, he didn't appear to feel the need to fill in the silence.

"Do you remember when the bakery was around?" she said.

"Yeah. It closed about ten years ago."

"Were the donuts good?"

"Everything was good. There just weren't enough people in this town to keep it going. The last I heard, their daughter had gone to Paris to study patisserie or something fancy like that, but that was years ago. Marie was her name. Why?"

"Nothing. I was just wondering." A small happy glow filled her that maybe her vision of a young Greyson had been true after all.

They stopped in front of what had, at first glance, seemed like an old house. Whoever owned it obviously took pride in it, the white picket fence starkly white against the gray of the evening. Suzie looked at him in confusion. *Didn't he say it wasn't family? Why were they going to someone's house?*

"Ma has been around forever. She always used to have a pot on of something or other. Anyway, folks reckoned she should sell the food, and that is how Ma's Diner came about. It's unlike any diner you've ever been to." He held the door for her expectantly and, curious, she entered the welcoming glow.

"Greyson Bedford, while I live and breathe. It's been how long since you've last been at my door?" A large gray-haired woman waddled forward, ladle in hand.

"Too long, Ma," Greyson mumbled, swallowed by the woman's generous proportions as she pulled him into an embrace. Suzie bit back a smile at the sight of the tall cowboy looking for all the world like a schoolboy being scolded.

"And who is this young lady? I'd know if she was from around here." Suzie found herself on the receiving end of a sharply appraising look.

"Ma, this is Suzie. She's a friend from out of town. Suzie, this is Ma, the owner of this fine establishment."

"The finest in this town, and that ain't saying much," Ma sassed. "You kids take that table over there." She pointed to a gingham covered table for two with mismatching chairs that stood slightly to one side of the open style kitchen she'd just come from. "I'll get you both a plate." Without further ado, she strode back to kitchen, the queen of her domain.

"But we didn't order," Suzie whispered as she sat in the chair Greyson held out for her, fearful she would offend the majestic Ma.

"That's not how Ma does it." He carefully unfurled the napkin and placed in on his lap. "She serves whatever she cooked today, and that depends on ingredients she's been able to get, the season, what the moon's doing. Oh, and I should warn you, Ma expects good table manners."

The words were no sooner out of his mouth when Ma returned with two steaming plates heaped with collard greens, meatloaf, mash, and biscuits. A teenage girl trotted behind her carrying glasses and a pitcher of pink lemonade. "Maddie, just put that down there," she instructed. "This is my granddaughter, Maddie."

"Hello, Maddie." Suzie smiled at the girl, who couldn't be more than fifteen at a guess.

"I love your hair," Maddie said as she carefully deposited her load on the table. "Is it hard to keep that color?"

Suzie's hand went to her hair. "I have to freshen it up otherwise it goes a yucky washed-out color, but I change my hairstyle all the time, so I don't really notice it."

"Now, leave them alone. Can't you see Greyson is on a date?" Ma gave the plate in front of Suzie a final straighten and, satisfied, shooed her granddaughter away.

Suzie tried not to smile as Greyson turned a bright shade of red. "I'm sorry. Ma sometimes makes assumptions."

"I'm fine with that assumption." A shy smile made Greyson look adorably cute. "How about we just go with it?" Picking up her fork, she hovered it over her plate. "Any suggestions on where to start?"

"It's all good, but I start with the greens."

"Get your vegetables out of the way?" Suzie couldn't resist teasing.

That smile again. It made her belly flutter in a way it hadn't for a long time. At least, it hadn't in a long time till she'd seen him at the reunion. "Something like that."

She took a bite, using her tongue to capture where some of the seasoning had fallen on her bottom lip. Suzie looked up to catch him staring at her like a starved man. *Well, well.* "It's good. I was thinking that I might be in the mood for something naughty after this."

His Adam's apple bobbed as he swallowed. "Yeah?" The way he was looking at her, it was like he'd never desired something so much in his life. Frankly, it was the same way she looked at chocolate.

"Yeah, and I hope you don't break my heart by telling me it won't happen." Greyson sat still, barely moving, his entire attention riveted to her. Suzie gave him a mischievous grin. "Please tell me that Ma has dessert and that it's as good as this."

Slowly, the tension drained from the cowboy's body and a wry half-smile ghosted the corners of his mouth as disappointment shadowed the depths of his eyes. Clearly he'd thought *she* had a different idea of naughty. A shiver of desire danced along her spine. *He wants me more than he lets on.* It made Suzie feel powerful and protective of Greyson at the same time. Here was a heart that could easily be broken.

"Maybe we could share?" she offered.

"I'd like that." They ate in silence for a moment longer until he paused to gaze at her intently. "You never did tell me what you've been up to all those years since we last saw each other. Not that I really got much of a chance to talk to you back then."

Suzie found herself telling him about her life and found, to her amazement, that he was completely non-judgmental of her choices along the way. He might not say much, but he was an incredible listener. And considering she was a talker, it was a match made in heaven.

All too quickly, the meal was over and she found herself being walked back to her motel. When they reached her door, she stood with her hand poised on the doorknob. "Thank you for a wonderful evening."

"It's my pleasure. It's the least I could do after you brought my favorite hat back to me. I reckon I didn't mention it before, but you sure did look good in it." Suzie could feel her cheeks glow pleasantly under his compliment.

"Do you think maybe you might want to do this again sometime—if we're ever in the same place again?"

"I'd like that, Greyson. I'd like that a lot."

He smiled his shy smile as they stood for a moment that stretched out between them, Suzie unsure if he would kiss her goodnight or not. And then, with a nod of his head and a murmured goodnight, he was gone. Disappointment quickly evaporated as she gazed appreciatively at his snug denim clad derriere sauntering away from her. Suzie knew what she'd be dreaming about tonight.

FOUR WEEKS TILL CHRISTMAS

"I think you corrupted me," Suzie said, staring out the window to the street below her apartment as she talked on the phone. "I thought I could fight it, but I was wrong. I don't think I want to fight this feeling anymore."

"And I'm supposed to be the dramatic one." Veronica laughed. "Is it really that hard to admit that you're looking forward to the cold?"

"But I've never liked the cold in my life. It's actually why my therapist says I'm experiencing conflicting emotions." She hadn't felt the need to tell her therapist about the shy cowboy in Texas yet.

"If it makes you feel better, isn't Christmas meant to be filled with snow, roaring fires and cups of hot cocoa?"

"You've got me. Now, I've got a few gifts for Lulu, but is there anything she needs or has said she'd like?" Suzie couldn't wait to see her little offsider.

"The child lacks for nothing, believe me. She has started moving away from her pink phase. She still loves her unicorns, but seems to like wearing black with them."

Suzie laughed. "I knew that girl had style. There's a black tutu I've had my eye on for her. Then we can be matching."

Veronica snorted. "Just what Hank always wanted. Now, has your cowboy called yet?" Suzie had filled her in on all the details as soon as the door had closed behind her that night. *Pity there hadn't been much more to add since.*

Suzie felt an instant squeezing hurt. "No. I don't know if I was reading that night wrong or not. I mean, I know he isn't like most of the guys I've met before, but he really is like this old-fashioned gentleman wrapped up in this gorgeous, hot guy body. And I thought there was something—some chemistry—between us." Suzie swallowed past the lump that lingered in her throat. "And he was such a good listener too."

Veronica chuckled. "Which is good, since you're such a good talker." Her voice grew serious. "Why don't you just call him and put yourself out of your misery?"

Suzie whirled away from the window, her actions animated. "Because I traveled all the way to Texas to give him his dang hat back. The least he can do is make an effort and call me."

"Easy," soothed Veronica. "It was only a suggestion. Now, let me tell you what I'm getting Hank for Christmas. You're going to love it. I'm not sure if he will, but I've got some other things for him so I don't have all my eggs in the one basket." Pensively, Suzie stared outside again, wondering what could have happened since she'd seen Greyson last. *Dang it. Why hasn't he called?*

Did she want him to call? Maybe she was just being friendly, and he was reading too much into it. Greyson had never met a woman like Suzie before. She was gorgeous and funny and smart as a whip. She probably had guys throwing themselves at her all the time. Guys with something to offer. What would a woman like her want with a poor cowboy who couldn't even afford a new pair of jeans? Like she'd really want someone like him to call her.

And yet, he couldn't pull his eyes away from her number on his phone. *But what if she does want you to call?* his mind taunted him.

"Hey, idiot, why haven't you fixed the water pipe to the front paddock yet? It ain't gonna fix itself."

Ain't that the truth. Greyson carefully put his phone in his pocket. "Actually, I'm glad you said something. I could use a hand—make the job go faster."

Bronson curled his bottom lip like he'd just smelled something offensive. "It's raining out there. I ain't helping." Greyson stared at him, anger making his spine straight. "Something you want to say? Cause if you ain't happy, you know where the front door is. Heck, Rob and I have been better to you than we've had to, considering you ain't no kin of ours."

For the millionth time, Greyson wanted to throttle his dearly departed father. Why had he seen fit to leave the ranch to his new wife? Lust-fueled stupor seemed the most likely. But then to have her die and leave everything to her sons... The betrayal slammed hard into him again. Dad had given away his home. The one Mom had loved with all her soul. Maybe that was why he couldn't leave it. To leave would mean that it had never really been theirs at all. Grabbing a rain jacket from a hook, he marched out the door, damning the old man with every breath he took.

Greyson knew Suzie was out of his league. He knew that she probably wasn't thinking about him, but dang if he could get her out of his mind.

"Emma, she's like the prettiest rainbow you've ever seen. You know, like the ones on the posters that have a waterfall or an impossibly green meadow and a rainbow that is so ethereal that it could only exist in heaven? That's what Suzie is like, but with a little more punch to her."

Greyson draped his arm around Emma as she ate, not minding in the least that, except to look at him with large liquid eyes, she didn't join in the conversation. *Emma is like that.*

"I know what you're thinking. All you've heard about all week is Suzie this and Suzie that. Dude just needs to man up and call her, but I've been guzzling milk all week just to stop my belly from getting an ulcer." Emma continued to stare at him. "Now, don't look at me like that. She's the kind of girl who's worth getting all twisted up in knots about. But I've left it so long that maybe it would be awkward if I called now. Like, would she even remember who I am?"

He could have sworn he saw judgment in her eyes. Ignoring her, he reached down and took a slug from the bottle at his feet.

"How about we forget about Suzie for a bit and just enjoy the moment. Bronson and Rob will be headed into town soon. Ain't like they're going to let a Friday night go by without going to a bar." He sighed, giving the cow a pat. "And before you say anything, I'm not hiding out here either."

Clearly having lost interest in the conversation, Emma sauntered away to get a drink, leaving him to his thoughts that, this time, he swore wouldn't be about Suzie.

SHOCK RIPPLED through Suzie as she stared at the number on her phone. *Greyson!* She pursed her mouth for a moment. *Maybe he'd accidentally pocket dialed or something?* Only one way to find out. "Hello?"

"Hello, is this Suzie?" There was a relaxed tone to Greyson's voice, warm and syrupy.

"It is. Were you hoping for someone else?" she replied archly. Look, she liked the guy, but he'd made her wait before calling and he didn't deserve to get off completely.

"Nope, you're exactly who I was hoping for. Ain't ever hoping for anyone else." *Okay, the boy was smooth.*

Suzie cleared her throat, pretending to not be affected, even if his words left a flattered warmth behind. "I'm actually surprised to hear from you. I kinda assumed you'd lost my number."

A slow chuckle greeted her words. "I'm sorry. To be honest, it was a process to get to this point."

Now that hurt. "A process to get to calling me? I'm sorry that it was so difficult."

"I wasn't sure if you wanted me to call. But it turns out I wanted to talk to you more than I feared rejection."

Suzie couldn't recall the last time a man had ever been quite so honest. "Of course I wanted you to call. Why would I give you my number if I didn't?"

"Maybe because you were just being nice."

"Greyson, I am nice, but only to a point. And there is no way I would give my number to a man who I didn't want to call me."

"It does sound a little silly when you put it like that."

"Well, good. Don't make the same mistake, do you hear?"

There was that chuckle again—the one that did all sorts of funny things to her tummy. "Yes, ma'am."

"Good. So, how has your week been?"

"Busy. Winter on a ranch always is."

Suzie settled in on the sofa, pulling a blanket over her as she tucked her legs under herself. "We found that out last year."

"You have a ranch?" Disbelief made Greyson's voice go up several notches.

A giggle escaped Suzie at his stunned amazement. "Well, I don't. But last Christmas, my friend, Veronica—I think I mentioned her when we last spoke?" They'd spoken, or more precisely, she'd spoken about such a broad range of topics when they'd had dinner that she couldn't imagine that Veronica hadn't come up. "She bought a ranch in Wyoming just over a month before Christmas and we had zero ranching experience. Thank goodness for Hank, Veronica's now fiancé. Not that we'd admit it, but we would have been in way over our heads without him. That's where I'm spending Christmas again this year. It's the best. And I've already got most of the gifts sorted, but Lulu can always have more."

"Who's Lulu?"

"Hank's daughter and my official sidekick, offsider and best friend for life."

"She sounds cool."

"You have to meet her. She really is." It occurred to her that, once again, he was doing most of the listening. "What are your plans for Christmas?"

"It's not all that different from any other day on the ranch for me."

Shocked, Suzie blinked. *How could Christmas be just like any other day?* "But you live on the family ranch, don't you?"

"That's how it started, yeah." His voice was utterly devoid of emotion.

"How it started? Then what is it now?"

"How it is now is that my stepmom left the ranch to my stepbrothers. And they usually find some girl or another to feel sorry for them on Christmas and invite them over for dinner."

"But what about you?"

"You might not have noticed, but I don't really have a way with the ladies, and I guess I kinda just think about what it was like when Mom was alive and even Dad before he remarried. My mom loved Christmas. She'd spend all week baking and planning. Heck, decorating the house started as soon as it was December, and she'd be singing carols at the top of her lungs. Man, she couldn't hold a note, but what I'd give to hear her one more time."

A lump formed in Suzie's throat at the naked longing in his voice. "She sounds amazing."

"She was."

The silence wasn't awkward. Instead, Suzie could almost feel Greyson on the other end, wrapped in memories. "Would you like to talk about her?"

A hesitation. *Maybe it was too soon to be so personal.* "Her name was Rose, and she smelled like vanilla and she was always dancing."

Suzie smiled. "And did you dance with her?"

"Yeah. She'd grab my hands, and we'd dance around the room. When I was little, she'd hold me on her hip and do it."

"Maybe one day you could show me some of the moves she showed you."

And another pause. "I'd like that."

A connection, somehow spanning the distance between them, tugged her to him. "I'd like that too."

TWO WEEKS TILL CHRISTMAS

*O*ne week—*was that all it had been?* A week of nightly talks that went well into the wee hours of the morning filled with anything and everything that crossed their minds. Suzie did feel a bit bad that she might be responsible for Greyson not getting a lot of sleep, what with the early wake-up call of a rancher.

"It will be so nice to be back home at the ranch. These whirlwind seventy-two-hour world promotional tours are killers." Veronica sounded exhausted. "I miss Hank and Lulu."

Suzie pulled her mind back to the phone conversation. "Heck, I miss Hank and Lulu and I don't even live at the ranch," Suzie retorted. She couldn't wait to head down for Christmas. *Not long now.*

"I'm amazed you have time for missing anyone with all the phone calls with Greyson," her friend teased. "Not that I can tell, what with all the Greyson this and Greyson that. Girl, you have it bad."

Suzie blushed, she had been talking an awful lot about Greyson, but she couldn't help it. He was her new favorite topic. "I thought I hid it well."

Veronica snorted. "You're clearly delusional if that's what you thought. Anyway, I think it's cute. And time for payback after all the fun you had with me and Hank last year."

"I was helping you and Hank last year."

"Is that what you called it?" Veronica chuckled. "Well, it did help, and since you showed me how to do it, I'm all prepared to return the favor this Christmas. Phone calls are nice and all, but when are you going to see him next?"

Suzie reached for her cup of tea. Somehow, in all their conversations, neither of them had ever quite managed to bring it up. "We haven't really talked about it."

"Poor guy is probably too busy trying to get a word in edgewise. How about this. Since the ranch brought me such good luck last year, you invite him down here to spend Christmas with us. Might as well show him what he's in for if he becomes part of our family."

A buzz of excitement coursed through her. "I like how you think."

"Does that mean you'll ask him?"

Suzie nibbled her bottom lip. "I will when I speak to him tomorrow." *But would he say yes?*

THE PHONE WAS STILL warm in Greyson's hands as he stared at it in disbelief. Suzie wanted to spend Christmas with him. He mentally started running through a list of things he'd have to do before he left and, of course, his brothers would have to do his share of things while he was away. *But still, Christmas with Suzie. Wow, wow, wow!* Heart singing, he heaved the last bale of hay into place. Might as well tell them now. The sooner he told them, the sooner he could start packing. He found them where he knew he would. Feet up on the coffee table, watching the basketball game on the television.

"Guys, can I have a moment?"

"Only if it's because you're bringing beer." Rob waggled an empty bottle at him.

"Well, no." Greyson hated how his voice stammered.

"Then no." Bronson answered for his brother.

"It's important." Greyson planted his feet firmly into the threadbare carpet. "I'm going away for Christmas, so you need to help out around the ranch."

That caught their attention. Rob turned, brow raised insultingly. "Where do you think you're going?"

"More to the point, who would want to spend time with him?" Bronson sneered.

"Suzie has invited me to spend Christmas with her at her friend's ranch." Greyson's chest puffed out proudly. *There, take that!*

"You're telling me that Suzie wants you to hang around with her and her fancy-pants friends. Isn't one of them a movie star or something?" Rob slapped his thigh as he let out a barking laugh. "As if."

"I mean, look at him." Bronson elbowed his chortling brother. "I don't reckon his truck will even make it that far."

"There must be something wrong with that girl Suzie if she wants to ruin her Christmas by spending it with you." Rob rubbed where his brother had been a little too enthusiastic with his jabs. "Maybe she feels sorry for you."

Nausea swam in Greyson's belly, threatening to pull him into its vortex of despair. *What if they were right?* Not about Suzie, she was perfect. Maybe he was just a pity case. Shoulders slumped, he turned, escaping his tormentors as he fled the room.

~

THE RINGING SEEMED OVERLY loud in his ear, matching the pounding of his heart. Greyson swallowed, trying to force some moisture back into his throat.

"Hello, gorgeous." He almost dropped the phone at Suzie's energetic greeting.

Did she really think he was gorgeous? Doubtfully, he looked down at his mud-splattered clothes. "Um, hi, Suzie."

"I wasn't expecting you to call until tonight, but I'm sure glad you surprised me early. Let me just find a quiet spot to talk."

He swallowed again, his tongue suddenly feeling like it didn't belong in his mouth. "If it's not a good time to talk, I can call back."

"Don't be silly." He heard a door close. "That's better. How have you been?"

"Good. You?"

"So ready for my Christmas holiday."

"That's actually what I was calling about." *Tell her.*

"That you're looking forward to it, too? It's going to be so much fun. I know you'll like Veronica and Hank."

"Ah, more that I don't think I can come. The ranch … you know."

"Oh." There was a sad catch in her voice. "I understand. Everyone was so excited to meet you." A pause, and then she spoke softly. "I was excited to see you."

It hit him like a ton of bricks. He wasn't a pity case to her. She actually wanted to see him. This amazing girl wanted to spend Christmas with HIM! Greyson hated that he'd let his stepbrothers get to him, to twist something so pure into something he doubted. "You know what? I reckon my stepbrothers can look after it. Now that I think about it, that's the perfect solution. How about I come down a little earlier—if you like." *Where had this confidence come from?* "Maybe we could do some things together and just hang out." Heck, this was the most words he'd ever strung together.

"You mean that?" The way her voice changed, the delighted anticipation animating her, it swirled around his heart, warming it.

"Sounds like you're going to be seeing me sooner than you reckoned."

Suzie clapped her hands on the end of the phone. "Talk about from a low to a high." As she excitedly chattered away, Greyson made a vow to himself to never let his stepbrothers sabotage him again. Or himself, for that matter.

ONE WEEK TILL CHRISTMAS

*A*s soon as Suzie had turned the car onto the long gravel drive—*or was it better to call it a road?*—she'd wound down her window, breathing the crisp air in, glorying in the way her lungs fully expanded. There was something about the Wyoming air that felt like she could truly breathe. Excitement mingled with a sense of home as, once again, the lodge rose up in front of her against a backdrop of trees in their winter finery.

Lulu was out the door before she'd even managed to turn her car off—Suzie had caught sight of her peeking from the window—Hank trailing behind her with a hearty greeting and promises to get her bags. With her favorite sidekick beside her, Suzie was settled in on the sofa with a warm cup of cocoa before she'd had time to say "Deck the Halls."

Speaking of which... Looking around, her brow crinkled at the distinct lack of a tree. Sure, there were decorations, but not the centerpiece taking pride of place. "Um, Veronica, you do know it's traditional to have a Christmas tree, right?"

"I was waiting for Veronica to come home before we went and picked one," Hank said, using his hip to close the door behind him. He kind of had to, considering he had a bag hanging from their straps off each shoulder and a suitcase in each hand. "How long are you staying again?"

"A girl needs to come prepared." Suzie touched her red-and white-striped dyed hair. "And you wouldn't want me to not look my best."

"You look beautiful." Lulu gazed adoringly up at her. *How was she four already?* "Mommy Vee, Daddy, can I have hair like that?"

"No!" both parents said in alarmed unison.

"Maybe when you're older and you come and visit Auntie Suzie," she promised, winking at the not-so-little girl. She turned her perplexed expression back to the grown-ups. "But that still doesn't explain why you don't have a tree. Veronica has been back for a week."

"When she got home, Veronica didn't want you to miss out on the tree picking," Hank said over his shoulder as he made his way up the stairs.

Love for her friend flowed through her as her eyes moistened. "Come here." Suzie held her arms open wide and pulled Veronica into a hug. "You're the best. You know that, right?"

"I was pretty confident I am," Veronica replied modestly as she settled back onto the sofa.

"Well, you are my friend, so you have to be." Suzie picked up her cup again. "When do you want to go get one then? It just doesn't feel like Christmas without the tree."

"Now that I think about it," Veronica began slowly, an idea obviously just coming to her given the pleased expression that danced across her famous face. "Should we wait for Greyson now?"

Suzie smiled happily back. "I like the way you think."

〜

THE STEERING WHEEL was slick beneath Greyson's hands, the doubts he'd spent the entire drive trying to ignore growing stronger. Strangely, they'd taken on his stepbrothers' sneering voices. Seeing the gates for Suzie's friend's ranch, he turned, driving through them. It might not have been the fastest or the smoothest ride, but his old truck had made it. Greyson patted the dash. "Good girl."

His heart accelerated as he took in the pristine state of the ranch outside his truck, so at odds with his home. *Was that bison?* It took all of his self-control to not turn around when he saw the sheer scale of the lodge up ahead of him. Had he made a mistake coming here? Greyson swallowed, trying to ease the dryness in his mouth. He'd come all this way to spend Christmas with Suzie and he was sure as heck going to do that, no matter how much he wanted to tuck his tail between his legs. Because she was worth pushing through the fearsome nerves that rattled his backbone.

Parking and getting his single bag from his truck took less time than his frayed emotions would have liked, and then he was standing facing the massive timber front door running through a mental pep talk. Raising his fist to knock, he jerked back in surprise when the door opened before he could, revealing a man with a small smile twitching at the corners of his mouth.

"I reckon you were almost going to freeze to death before you got around to knocking. I'm Hank." He held his hand out.

Greyson returned the firm handshake, letting out a soft snort as he entered the warmth of the lodge. There was something about Hank's easygoing demeanor that set him at ease immediately. "It might have been on the cards."

"I can't have that happening. Can you imagine the weeping and wailing I'd have to put up with from the ladies? It would spoil Christmas." Hank closed the door against the bracing cold of outside. "Suzie, ya man's here," he called over his shoulder.

Is *that how* everything thought of him? *Suzie's man.* It had a nice ring to it.

She was a vision as she came running out of the other room. But then, she always had been whenever he'd been lucky enough to lay eyes on her. The gentle shade of lavender that he'd spent the better part of a month fantasizing about what it would feel like to run his fingers through was now a startling candy cane themed concoction. And yet, she was still the most beautiful thing he'd ever seen.

"Greyson, I'm so glad you're here," she said as she pulled him into a ferocious hug. *She even smells like a candy cane.*

"Me too. There were times I didn't think the old truck would make it." He awkwardly nodded at the tall, beautiful woman who glided into the room like a queen to stand beside Hank, a young girl peering at him from behind them. "Hello, I'm Greyson."

A warm smile softened her face. "I'm Veronica, and this"—she patted the girl's head—"is Lulu, and I'm afraid she is a little jealous that you're stealing the attention of her best friend."

Greyson knew how it felt to have the person who lit up your world suddenly taken away from you. He knelt down until he was eye level with the stormy-faced little girl. "Suzie's pretty amazing, isn't she?"

Lulu eyed him suspiciously. "Yeah."

"I think so, too. But you were her best friend first. Do you think maybe you could share her with me? I promise not to steal her all her time."

The little girl chewed the idea over, her expression not giving an inch. "I get to sit on her lap when we hand out presents."

"Deal."

"I'm on her team when we bake."

Greyson had no idea what teams had to do with baking. "Sure."

Was it his imagination or was Lulu softening a little? "You can help her read stories to me if you like."

"I'd like that."

"Now, if you've finished interrogating Greyson, can you please let Suzie show him to his room?" Veronica gave him an apologetic smile as he rose to his feet again. "I'm sorry about that."

"Don't be. I reckon I'd be just the same if she was my best friend."

There was a glow to Suzie's cheeks. Clearly, she liked the idea of him being her friend. "Now that everyone's met, I'll show you to your room."

She grabbed hold of his hand and began leading him away before he could get another word in. Not that he had much more left to say. He'd almost used up his quota for the moment. Her hand felt delicate, but oddly strong at the same time. Like what he imagined touching a wild cat would be like. After going up some stairs, she stopped in front of a door.

"This is your room. My room is across the hall, Lulu's is beside mine, and Hank and Veronica's is at the end. If you like, I can give you a chance to settle in." Suzie stood there, an eagerness glittering in her eyes.

"No need. Just need to stash my bag and then I'll come back down with you." He pushed open the door to the largest bedroom he'd ever set foot in, let alone slept in. The large window framed with inky navy curtains opened out to a view of the valley, giving the room an ethereal quality. Everything screamed of understated wealth and luxury, even if it still had a ranch vibe. Greyson hesitated in putting his bag down, fearful it would leave a mark. He glanced around, wondering if he could leave it in the bathroom.

"Is everything okay?" Suzie asked, eyeing him expectantly.

Mentally promising himself he'd come back and clean up any mess later, he placed his bag just inside the door. "No, just taking it all in."

"It's pretty amazing, isn't it? When Veronica decided she was going to buy a ranch last year, this was not what I was expecting at all." Suzie happily chattered as she led him back down the stairs. "But then again, I shouldn't have been surprised. Veronica does like the finer things in life."

"Who likes the finer things in life?" Hank asked as they entered the room.

"Veronica," Suzie said, plonking herself down on one of the tan sofas.

The woman in question patted her fiancé on the thigh. "Does that mean you're one of the finer things, too?" she asked him sweetly.

"Reckon I must be, since I know how much you like me." Hank winked at her as he placed his hand over hers. They were clearly in love.

Greyson looked around the room. For a room the size it was, it had still somehow retained a cozy feeling to it. The fire cheerfully flickered in the fireplace, the mantle draped with Christmas stockings. A brightly colored glass bowl sat on the coffee table filled with candy canes and other assorted Christmas themed candies. Tastefully arranged holiday ornaments were scattered about the room. Greyson frowned as he noticed for the first time the absence of a Christmas tree. *Maybe they had a special room just for that.* Who knew with movie stars. Maybe they did things a bit differently to other folk.

"Did you just notice we don't have a tree?" Suzie asked

with a giggle. "At least, that's what it looks like from the expression on your face."

"I was wondering." He trailed off.

"They were waiting for everyone to get here to help pick a tree. Now that you're here, we can get one tomorrow." Greyson lost himself in those liquid eyes as she looked at him.

"Be good to have another man around to help," Hank said. "Not that I'm complaining about being the rose amongst the thorns." He ducked as the women threw cushions at him. Lulu quickly copied, launching one at her father. "On that note, would you like a coffee?"

"Sounds good." Greyson wasn't quite sure what to do with his hands. Suzie took one in hers, solving that problem for him. His anxiety lessoned at the gentle stroking of her thumb on the back of his hand.

"Suzie said you both met when she was doing her first movie," Veronica said, picking up her own cup to take a sip. "I think it was the first one she'd worked on."

Greyson glanced at Suzie in surprise. "It was?"

Suzie nodded. "Yep, sure was."

"I wasn't even going to put my name down to be an extra, but I'm glad I did." The way Suzie's smile lit up made his belly do funny things.

"What made you put your name down?" Veronica asked curiously as she wrapped an arm around Lulu.

"My mom, when she was alive, liked to act and was in a few local productions. She signed me up for a few too. Reckon she thought it would help with my self-confidence." Greyson flashed a shy smile. "I'm not sure it worked. After she died, well, I didn't do it anymore." He didn't add how stupid his stepbrothers had made him feel for being a sissy actor. "The day I saw the flyer wanting ranch hands as extras for the movie they were filming in town, well, that was

Mom's birthday. I reckon she wanted me to do it, a little push from heaven." Greyson was surprised at how easily he was sharing his story. The words flowing from him. "I'm also a Luciano Navarro fan and thought that maybe I'd get a chance to meet him. So, I put my name down, and the rest is history." He smiled down at Suzie. "I'm glad I did."

Suzie squeezed his hand, her cheeks a dusky pink as she returned his look. "Me too."

SOMEHOW, and Suzie wasn't quite sure how, Lulu had flipped her opinion and now considered Greyson her new boyfriend too. In the back seat of Hank's truck, he sat in the middle seat holding Suzie's hand and, after Lulu had noticed, now sat holding the little girl's hand as well. She wasn't sure she'd ever liked him more. *He really is a sweetheart.* That aside, every bump they went over forced their thighs to touch, and as innocent as it was to sit holding hands, her thoughts had strayed far from it. When the truck finally stopped, she didn't know whether she was thankful the delicious torture had stopped or upset.

Taking charge, Hank looked around at the stand of trees they were in as he pulled on a thick pair of gloves. "Anyone see one they like the look of?"

Veronica went and stopped beside a gigantic fir. "This one might fit."

"In a castle," Suzie snorted. "I mean, the lodge is huge and all, but that thing is gigantic."

"This one." Lulu was beside an oddly misshapen specimen.

"Um, maybe we can keep looking?" suggested Hank diplomatically. "This one is about the right size." He appraised the tree in question. "And looks to be easy enough to get down. What do you think, Greyson?"

"It seems like a good one," Greyson agreed.

"I think Lulu's one is kinda cute," Suzie interrupted.

"It looks like a grizzly bear decided to use it as a toothpick," Hank argued. "This one is better."

"It gives it character," Veronica stepped up protectively beside the tree.

"This family has enough character as it is. Now that's settled"—Hank ignored the angry glares headed his way and went back to the truck to retrieve his chainsaw—"you want to give me a hand, Greyson?"

"I'll give him high and mighty," muttered Veronica, bending down to scoop up a handful of snow and rolled it into a ball. She launched it with all her might, hitting her fiancé square in the back of the head.

"Hey!" bellowed Hank.

"Nice throw," complimented Suzie as she threw her own snowball, laughing as the men ran for cover behind the truck.

"Thank you. It's good to know all that training I did for the Baseball Babes wasn't for nothing." Veronica ducked to one side. "We might want to consider a more defensive position."

A snowball hit Suzie in the chest. She looked up to see Greyson's wide-eyed face appear on the other side of the truck. "Sorry," he called.

"Oh, this means war," Suzie retorted. "And I don't care how cute you look, I'm taking this personally."

What followed was an intense, albeit brief, skirmish. Neither sides were quite sure who emerged victorious.

Actually, that wasn't quite true. As Lulu was lifted high in the air later to place the tin star on the perfectly imperfect tree that had started it all, it was quite clear the little girl had won.

Greyson's arm was stretched along the back of the sofa and, seizing her opportunity, Suzie snuggled into him. She could have sworn he held his breath for a second before letting it drape around her shoulders. From her warm cocoon, she watched the final decoration being added. "Remember when we almost lost that star last year?"

"All I can say is he's very lucky he returned it," rumbled Hank.

"How is Anton going?" Suzie asked. "I haven't heard about him for ages."

"Last I heard, he was narrating a documentary for elementary school kids about paper," Veronica said smugly.

"Looks like he's the only fake star who got thrown out in the trash." Suzie laughed. A delicious languidness turned her bones to mush. Maybe she could just stay like this forever, melted into Greyson's side, surrounded by friends with Christmas carols in the background. The question was, how was she going to get Greyson to stay past the holidays?

SIX DAYS TILL CHRISTMAS

The street had a constant flow of people looking for the perfect last minute Christmas gift as Suzie guided Greyson inside the shop. The bell on the door tinkled as they stepped into the warmth. Taking her gloves off, she looked about her with an air of contentment. "In here, it is Christmas all year round."

"Doubly so when it's actually the holidays." A gray-haired man, eyes sparkling merrily from behind his glasses, walked out from behind the counter to pull Suzie into a hug. "How's my favorite Christmas helper?"

"In my element." She looped her arm through Greyson's. "Mr Peterson, this is Greyson. Greyson, this is Mr Peterson, who might just have the best job in the world."

"Pleased to meet you, Mr Peterson," Greyson said, looking around at all the Christmas paraphernalia. "I can see why Suzie likes it in here. You've got a lot of cool stuff."

"I do try." Mr Peterson blew out his cheeks happily, looking for all the world like a pleased chipmunk. "Now, is this just a visit to breathe in the Christmas spirit, or is there something in particular you're looking for?"

"Just breathing it all in," Suzie replied, happily snuggling into Greyson. She couldn't remember the last time a man made her feel so happily complete. And this was from a woman who only saw a man as the icing on the cake, not the complete dessert. *Merry Christmas to me.*

"Actually, there is something," Greyson said, surprising her. "Do you have any pickle ornaments?"

"I have a little selection of them." Mr Peterson pointed to the far corner of his shop. "You'll find them over there." Greyson thanked him quietly before heading in the direction indicated.

"Pickles?" she asked.

"Yeah, my mom always had a pickle ornament that she'd hide. I remember feeling so proud when I found it. Once she died, we never did it again. I'm not even sure where it went. Once Dad remarried, most of her stuff disappeared like she was never there." He might as well be talking about the stock exchange for all the emotion in his voice.

Suzie's heart wept for him. "Maybe we could pick one together, start a new tradition?"

Greyson's eyes were murky with emotion as he looked at her. *The guy needs to let it all out at some point. No good ever comes from bottling it all up.* "I'd like that."

Her heart flip-flopped in her chest at his shy smile. She picked up a large green glass ornament. "How about this one?"

"You can't make it too easy." His face was scrunched adorably in concentration. Greyson touched a smaller one. "And you can't make it too hard either."

"It's the same old pickle conundrum then."

He turned, frowning at her in confusion. "I don't understand."

"Not too big, not too small. Just right."

Greyson's face lightened as he smiled at her, looking less careworn. "It is a pickle."

THE LAST PIECE of machinery rumbled into the workshop as the sky turned a hazy gray, the sun setting on another wintery day. Greyson climbed down from the tractor, feeling comfortably at ease as he helped Hank with the ranch jobs.

"Thanks for your help today." Hank handed him a beer.

"Didn't feel right to be sitting in the house not helping." Greyson gladly accepted the offering. "I don't really like being inside doing nothing if I can help it."

"I know the feeling. Veronica likes to take me in town shopping with her and such. I don't mind too much, but I'm also real happy when Suzie comes to stay. They can do all that girly stuff and I can have some peace and quiet."

In the distance, Greyson could hear the cattle mooing as they jostled over the feed they'd spread out for them. He wondered how his stepbrothers were going with keeping on top of the chores back at home. The last few days helping out on the ranch with Hank, they'd formed an easy comradeship. Somehow the other man made him feel appreciated and that his skills were valuable.

"I appreciate you and Veronica welcoming me into your home for Christmas."

"Suzie is family to us, and if you're important to her, then you're important to us. I bet your family will miss you."

Greyson swallowed at the easy acceptance. What did they see in him? "I doubt it."

Hank's brows lowered over his baffled eyes. "But it's Christmas."

"We aren't what you would call the closest of families. Sometimes I feel like I'm only allowed to stay there so they don't have to pay someone to do my work." Bitterness left a hollow feeling in his chest.

"I'd pay good money for a worker like you."

Greyson looked at him to gauge whether the man was making fun of him or not. "I could do with the money. I'm tired of working my tail off and being poor all the time and treated like a dog. It would be nice to be someone Suzie would be proud to be seen with."

"If you think that's something that matters to Suzie, you don't know her very well. That girl dances to the beat of her own drum and she's crazy about you."

"It might not matter to her, but it matters to me. Maybe then I can actually pluck up the courage to tell her exactly how I feel about her."

"I reckon she knows you like her." Hank gave him a lopsided smile. "We all know you like her."

"It's more than that. I've never felt the same way about anyone that I do about her." He sighed. How did he explain his feelings? That somehow he felt lighter when she was around. That she felt like the sun, lighting up the dark parts of his soul. "She's special."

"That she is. But obviously, to invite you here, she thinks you're something special too." Hank drank the last of his beer. "And if I don't want to get a scolding from the special ladies in my life, we'd better head inside and get cleaned up. I hear the game of find the Christmas pickle is still being battled out." He peered at Greyson. "Where, exactly, did you hide it?"

Greyson smiled slowly back at his newfound friend. "I like you Hank, but not enough to tell you before I tell Suzie."

Hank's broad smile flashed in his tanned face as he clapped Greyson on his shoulder. "Wise man. Very wise man." Together in companionable silence, they went in search of their ladies.

FIVE DAYS TILL CHRISTMAS

*G*reyson had never realized how unhappy he had been before. Sure, he knew he wasn't in the best place mentally back home at the ranch. But somehow, here with people he'd only known for a few days, he felt carefree and content, making the depths that he'd plummeted to all the starker. He mulled it over as he set the table, Lulu following him seriously with him napkins.

It was clear that they all cared about each other. Hank and Veronica were obviously in a relationship, so it was to be expected, but it was more than that. They genuinely seemed to care about Suzie and, by extension, him. Greyson found his gaze straying to where Suzie was readying drinks for dinner. He chuckled to himself when he realized that she was singing a Christmas carol to herself as she worked. Hank made eye contact with him and jerked his head toward where Veronica was pulling dishes from the oven. It appeared the girls were involved in a duet.

Hank shook his head in mock dismay, Greyson giving him a shrug back. With a flourish, Suzie put the final garnish on the glasses. Still singing happily, she danced over to him, holding a drink in front of her. In one smoothly executed twirl, she somehow managed to put it into his hand before planting a kiss on his startled cheek and continuing on her way to deliver more. Didn't she know what that would do to him?

Greyson stared down at the red concoction she'd left. It was garnished with crushed candy canes around the rim, with one that had been saved from destruction left in to act as a swizzle stick. Slowly, his free hand crept to where her lips had been a moment before. A slow smile stretched his lips in wonderment.

"Be careful. They sneak up on you and steal your heart before you even know what they are doing. Those girls might just be the most dangerous things in all of Wyoming," Hank said slyly as he carried some dishes to the table.

Greyson didn't reckon he'd mind at all if Suzie stole his heart. The fact of the matter was, she probably already had. Shaking himself from her spell, he collected the rest of the dishes and followed Hank's lead. In a gaggle of laughter, singing and chatter, the family took their places. No sooner had he sat down when Suzie's warm hand crept into his, sending a warming shiver through him.

"Greyson," Hank said from the head of the table, pulling him away from the thrall that he was under. "Veronica and I were talking."

Were they going to ask him to leave? Had he down something wrong? His misery was like a physical pain. "I'll go get my things." Good Lord, he didn't want to lose Suzie's gentle touch.

Veronica's eyes darted to Hank in bewilderment before returning to him. "Why would you do such a thing?"

"No one's asking you to go anywhere. And if they did, I'd

be going right with you," Suzie said. "But seriously, no one's asking you to leave."

Greyson stared around the table, the realization that he'd embarrassed himself by jumping to the wrong conclusion burning through him. "I'm sorry. It's just that, in my experience, good things don't last all that long."

"Oh, Greyson, they really did a good job on you, didn't they?" Suzie flung an arm around him, and he breathed her in. "They better not come near me, or I'll give them more than they counted on."

He swallowed down the lump in his throat at her fierce words. Hank coughed to get their attention again. "We'd like to offer you a job here at the ranch. I liked what I saw, and you've got the work ethic and personality that I think I could work side by side with. Obviously, we would still need to discuss the details of pay."

Greyson opened and closed his mouth several times, all the air having left his lungs. Veronica looked at him in appeal. "Hank's a good judge of character, but so am I, and I can't think of someone we'd rather have as part of our lives here on the ranch than you. Do you think you'd like that, too?"

He took a steadying breath, wrapping a hand around his drink as if somehow the cold would prove that this wasn't some dream his wistful imagination had brewed up. "I'd like that. I'd like that a lot, ma'am."

Veronica rolled her eyes to laugh at Hank. "What is it with cowboys and not being able to call me by my name? Just Veronica will do."

"Thank you … Veronica," Greyson managed.

"Looks like you aren't going to be so hard to find anymore, Greyson." Suzie gave him a saucy wink. "Fair warning, I spend a lot of time here."

Hank groaned. "I didn't think about that. Now that the

guy Suzie has a crush on is going to be living here, we're never going to get rid of her."

Veronica smiled sweetly at her fiancé. "She might even make this her home base when she's not working."

Lulu clapped her hands together excitedly. "Greyson and Suzie are moving in!"

"Well, Greyson is." Suzie gave him a look that had all sorts of promises lurking in its depths. "At least, for now."

~

SUZIE TRIED to stifle her giggles with her mitten clad hands. "I just assumed. I'm so sorry. We can do something else if you'd prefer."

Greyson clung grimly to the edge of the ice skating rink. "It doesn't look that hard, but I've seen newborn foals steadier on their feet than I feel right now." Like a man facing certain doom, he let go. For a moment, nothing happened. He remained upright. To be fair, judging from his face, he was too scared to move a muscle, but upright, nonetheless. And then, in a great flurry of windmilling arms and legs, he collapsed in a pile. "Man down."

Suzie skated closer and, bracing her feet, helped pull him upright again. "Maybe we could get one of those little plastic penguin things for you. Just until you figure it out."

Greyson gave a disgusted look as a four-year-old glided by. "I'd rather die."

"If you keep falling on your head like that, you just might."

His eyes narrowed in a mock threatening look, setting her to giggling again. "Just because I can't get my hands on you right now, doesn't mean that I can't be patient and wait until we're off the ice."

Suzie's belly flip-flopped. Her shy boy was growing teeth! Heck if that didn't make him even more attractive. "I'll take my chances." And with a saucy smile, she skated out of reach.

Greyson edged himself along. "I thought Christmas was all about the spirit of giving and goodwill to man."

She smugly did a little pirouette just for his benefit. "It is."

"And aren't we awfully close to Christmas Eve? You should doubly be good to me." He stopped, a sly look crossing his face. "Doesn't Santa have a list? Wouldn't want you to end up on the naughty list."

Suzie hopped from foot to foot as she did lazy circles near him. "Santa and I are good. He knows that I'm always going to be a little naughty, but I make up for it by having a good heart and not doing anything that's on the really bad list."

Greyson had stopped his slow progress to gaze hotly at her. The man was going to get them both into trouble if he kept looking at her like that. "Now I'm curious to hear about these naughty things Santa is okay with."

Not even bothering to fight the magnetic pull, she glided easily over to him, stopping to face him, hand resting easily on the rail. "A girl can't give away all her secrets."

If he kept looking at her like that, her knees might collapse into a quivering mess. "Not even one?" He leaned in closer, his breath warm on her cheek.

"Well, I'm pretty sure he's okay with kissing."

The intensity in his eyes burned even brighter. "I'm relieved to hear that. I wouldn't want to end up on the naughty list myself." His gaze dropped to her lips.

It was happening. He was actually going to kiss her. His head dipped lower, and she closed her eyes, waiting for the moment his lips would caress hers. A muttered curse and a thud made them fly open again. Perplexed, she stared at Greyson sprawled on the ice for a moment before throwing her head back and letting out a great peal of laughter.

"I think you're safe for now."

"Safe is not what I was going for," he muttered darkly before joining in her merriment.

She gave him a saucy wink. "Better luck next time, cowboy," she said before gliding away from him. It looked like their first kiss would have to wait for another day. At this rate, she was going to have to ask Santa for help!

FOUR DAYS TILL CHRISTMAS

*G*reyson had lain awake long into the night, pondering the meaning of life. His life. His family ranch was the only home he'd ever known. He'd somehow tangled up the feeling of keeping the memories of his mother alive with staying close to the land she'd love. But she was dead, and it was time he allowed himself to live —*really* live.

Good Lord, but he wanted to live clutching greedily at everything that came his way, starting with the vibrant woman he'd almost kissed last night. *Darn ice skating.* He could feel his lips twist into a smile at the comical aspect of it all. If he'd known that skating was what was going to let him down, maybe he'd have spent more of his youth perfecting the skill.

Downstairs, he could already hear the sound of voices, light laughter and singing. These people here were something else. Something that he wanted to be more than he could ever admit to. Greyson closed his eyes and clasped his hands together. "Dear Lord—and Santa." Best get all the big men on the job. He was going to need all the help he could get. "We haven't been on the best speaking terms for a while, but I really need your help. At the very least, a Christmas miracle. I want this chance. Please give me a sign that it's not all going to be taken away."

His eyes flew open at the ring of his phone. Reaching for it, Greyson frowned at the number. Bronson was never awake this early. *Maybe he'd turned a new leaf with being responsible for the ranch.* "Hello?"

"Don't hello me. The tractor won't start. You need to come on back and get it going," Bronson snarled through the line.

"The parts are all in the workshop. If not, you'll have to call someone from town to fix it," Greyson replied calmly. Thank goodness his pounding heart and sweaty palms didn't show in his voice.

"What's going to happen is you're going to come back here right now and fix it," Bronson threatened. "If you know what's good for you."

It was like a bell went off somewhere and, in that moment, everything became crystal clear. "It took me a while, but I reckon I finally do know what's good for me. On the deed for that ranch, it's got your and your brother's names. Reckon that makes it your problem."

"You come and fix it, you hear, or you won't ever be welcome to step foot back on this ranch. Wouldn't that make your dearly departed Ma sad to know you abandoned it?" Bronson sneered.

Greyson's heart lifted. His *mom* loved that ranch, but she loved him more. She would have wanted him to happy. "Then I reckon I won't be coming back." Heck, it wasn't like he had anything of value there. His entire wardrobe was so sparse he'd packed it to come to the lodge. "Seems like we've got nothing left to discuss, and there are people waiting for me." Greyson knew that a place would be set waiting for him downstairs, his friends smiling as he entered, happy that he was there. "Goodbye." With relish, he hung up the phone on his spluttering stepbrother. Greyson looked skyward. "I reckon that was a pretty good sign. Thanks." He smiled. "And Mom, I reckon I've taken long enough to figure it all out. I love you." Pushing the covers back, his step had a spring to it as he headed to the door and his new life.

"I SAY we make it boys versus girls." Veronica winked at Lulu and Suzie, clearly wanting to be on the winning team.

"Creative versus construction." Hank nodded slowly. "Could be fun."

"Or we could pull names out of a hat?" suggested Greyson.

This wasn't going to do at all. Time to take matters into her own hands. "Couples, and Lulu can help each team as she wants and be the judge." Suzie looked down at her offsider. "But I'm kinda hoping you mainly want to help me and Greyson."

Hank wrapped an arm around Veronica. "What do you think, sweetheart? Want to show those two how it's done?"

Veronica picked up a wooden spoon from the kitchen bench. "You better believe we're going to show them how it's done."

Suzie tied her favorite Mrs Clause apron snuggly around her waist. "Bring it. Greyson and I are going to win."

Greyson leaned in close. "Is now a good time to tell you I've never made a gingerbread house in my life?"

"Actually, a good time would have been before I picked you for my team." Suzie patted Greyson's cheek gently. "Just teasing. Good thing I'm a good teacher then."

He looked down as he felt a tug on his shirt sleeve. "I can

show you." Lulu held out a bowl.

"That's true. Lulu knows a thing or two about gingerbread house making," Suzie agreed. "Now, let's get started."

In a flurry of flour, eggs and spices, the gingerbread dough was made, rolled out, cut to shape using the templates and placed in the oven.

"I'm going to need more eggnog over here," declared Suzie.

"Coming right up, Mrs Clause." Greyson put down the icing sugar he'd been weighing out and hurried off to the other side of the kitchen.

"Lulu, how are your dad and Veronica doing? Go have a look and come back and tell me." Lulu scampered off on her mission. This might just be the most ambitious design Suzie had ever come up with. It was not a house, it was a compound. And not just any compound, but the lodge, ranch hands' quarters, barn and workshop. Fingers crossed she'd gotten all the parts she needed.

Greyson handed her a mug of eggnog. "Veronica told me I didn't put enough bourbon in it, so I brought the bottle over just in case."

Darn but this man is a keeper. "I like the way you think." She took a sip. "And Veronica's right. Add a little more in there, cowboy." Another taste. *Perfection.*

"Are you guys always so competitive?" Greyson propped a hip against the kitchen counter. It was impossible to not notice his muscular thighs through the thin worn denim.

Suzie reluctantly dragged her eyes away from the arresting sight. *Is it getting hot in here?* "You should see when we bake Christmas cookies. It's all in fun though."

"I don't think I've ever had a Christmas quite like this." Greyson looked up at the timer. "We have five minutes before we need to get the gingerbread out of the oven, is there anything I need to do after the icing sugar?"

"We can make the royal icing while they cool down. We'll collect the candy while that's happening, too." She took another appreciative sip of her eggnog. Lulu, having forgotten her mission, was now sucking on a candy cane watching her father chop up candy. *Wonder what that's going to be for...* "I meant to ask, is everything all right?"

He looked completely startled by her question as though it had been a long time since someone had asked it. Suzie's heart squeezed at the implications. Without thought, she pulled him into a fierce hug. When she finally released him, Greyson gave her a baffled smile, his eyes vulnerable.

"What was that for?"

"Because I felt like it. Now answer the question. Is everything all right?"

He glanced down for a moment at the mess on the kitchen bench before once again locking eyes with her. That same vulnerability shone forth. "I think I'm going to be." The solemn way he pronounced it was like it was a vow.

The timer went off, breaking the connection. "Looks like we'd better get those out of the oven and get a wiggle on." Suzie put a pair of oven mitts decorated to look like Christmas stockings on her hands. "We've got an entire ranch to build!"

LATER THAT NIGHT, drowsy in front of the fire, sipping on hot cocoa as the girls debated over who's gingerbread house had reigned supreme, Hank upstairs putting Lulu to bed, it occurred to Greyson that it was actually rather nice to be happy. His gaze drifted to Suzie, her hair pulled into a messy bun that looked for all the world like Christmas candy. With the tree in the background, falling in love was even nicer.

THREE DAYS TILL CHRISTMAS

The morning had started with a sparkle of magic. Wrapped up in the glow of last night's revelations and the soothing balm that was the lodge, Greyson had woken up marveling at how Christmassy he felt. The vibe had continued at breakfast, the gingerbread houses still to be inspected with no clear winner having been decided. Suzie's —and make no mistake, he'd only done what he'd been told to do—was something to behold. Everything had been done to scale with a precision that was mindboggling. She'd even added little bison and elk that she'd sculptured out of fondant. Greyson was a practical man. He could fix an engine or mend a fence, but the level of creativity Suzie possessed and the skill to actually make it come to life blew him away. That pretty much summed up how he felt about Suzie all round.

"You guys did a good job, too," Suzie admitted. "I like how you did Santa's grotto and the little elves."

"There's a reason I became an actress and not a special effects guru." Veronica laughed. "Against anyone else, that gingerbread house would have been a winner."

"Babe, you went up against the best. Ain't no shame in losing." Suzie nudged her friend. "Anyway, Judge Lulu still hasn't decided which one she's planning on giving the prize to."

"Lulu"—Hank swung his daughter up onto the kitchen bench—"you know Daddy loves you very much."

"Really?" demanded Suzie, hands on hips. "You're going to play that card?" She handed a candy cane out to the little girl. "Lulu, you know who my favorite sidekick is?"

Veronica smoothly intercepted the candy. "And I think you should both leave her alone."

"It's okay. I like them fighting over me." The little girl smiled sweetly at the two startled grown-ups. Greyson had to cover his own smile. He didn't want to encourage the behavior, after all.

"Why you little scallywag." Hank picked Lulu up and swung her about. "Remember, Santa's watching."

"Somehow I feel like Santa would be impressed with her." Suzie came over and took Greyson's hand in hers. *How did she keep making it seem like the most casual thing in the world?* As soon as she touched him, all he could feel was her warmth, her closeness, and she didn't act the least bit affected. "I know I am."

"Well, on that note, I need to get these troublemakers into town. I believe there's a sleigh ride with our name on it," Hank said to Suzie and Greyson.

"I'd be lying if I didn't say that having this cowboy all to myself is exactly what I want." Greyson's face flamed as hotly as the fire in his belly at Suzie's words.

Veronica gave her friend a knowing smile. "Then I'm a good friend, because I expect to be quite a while. Hopefully the sleigh ride goes better this year than last." She gave her fiancé an arched look as they left.

"I thought they'd never leave," Suzie said, popping a candy into her mouth.

"What did you have in mind?" Seriously, that didn't sound as cliched in his head.

"Quite a few things, actually."

"Suzie, did you mean what you said the other night?" he said as casually as he could muster.

"I say a lot of things, so I might need a little more detail. But generally, I mean most things I say." She hopped up onto the bench, her legs crossed demurely at the ankles as she leaned forward, her eyes gleaming speculatively. "What was it that I said?"

Greyson cleared his throat. "I think maybe I need a glass of water first."

Her laughter tinkled out joyously. "Come on. I'm not that scary, am I?"

Prudently choosing not to answer, he filled up a glass of water, bringing it to his lips in preparation to drink.

"Greyson, we know you're in there," a familiar male voice roared, accompanied by pounding on the front door.

"You better come out if you know what's good for you," another familiar voice joined in.

"What on earth?" Eyes wide, Suzie jumped down, heading toward the ruckus.

"I think I should handle this. It's me they're calling for." Greyson put himself between the determined woman and his stepbrothers.

"You know them?" She stopped her march to look up at him, shocked, before her mouth dropped open. "It's them, isn't it?"

He nodded his head before turning back to the door and opening it. Greyson took a step outside. No way was he letting them set foot in the lodge. Startled, Bronson and Rob backed up. Suzie closed the door firmly behind her.

"I'm here. What do you want?" Greyson asked calmly. A detached part of his mind marveled at how well he was handling the situation. Christmas miracles and all that.

"What do we want?" Bronson mocked to his brother before turning back to Greyson. "What do we want? Looks like Santa's come early to someone and given him a set of–"

"There's a lady present," Greyson interrupted. "Get to the point."

Rob made a show of looking around. "Ain't see no lady here. Unless you're talking about that freak there."

Greyson had Rob's shirt clenched between his fists before he'd even thought about it. "What did you say?" he growled through clenched teeth. A white incandescent rage made the blood pound in his ears.

"Geeze, calm down. It's not like she's worth getting upset about." Bronson grabbed at Greyson's arm, trying to free his brother. "She's nothing but a two-bit wh—"

Bronson never did quite get around to finishing that sentence before Greyson dropped Rob and swung into his jaw, knocking Bronson flat on his behind. Rob landed a glancing blow on Greyson. Fueled by pure savage adrenaline, he didn't even feel it, quickly countering with a blow that landed Rob in the snow beside Bronson. The brothers looked at each other, shaking their heads before jumping to their feet to attack again.

"Stop!" Suzie charged between them and Greyson, her arms held wide. "You need to leave."

"Step aside if you don't want to get hurt," Bronson blustered.

"Touch her and you will need an ambulance," Greyson promised. Fury pumped through his vision at the threat to his woman.

"Trust me, if he lays a single finger on me, that's exactly where he's going to end up, but it won't be you doing it."

Suzie glowered at her would-be attacker. "I live in LA. I eat bigger thugs than you for breakfast. Now, if you don't want to get hurt, you better get right back in that truck of yours and head back to where you came from."

"Come on." Rob grabbed his brother's arm. "It's his loss."

"Here we were, coming all the way from Texas to show you a little Christmas spirit and say we forgive you and you can come back to the ranch. Forget it now. You're never going to step foot on it again." Bronson spat on the snow beside him. "Don't come crawling back when she loses interest in you. You ain't welcome."

Watching his stepbrothers climb sullenly into their truck and then drive off, it struck him that he should be feeling a greater loss. But he was never going back to the ranch. Greyson wrapped his arm around Suzie's shoulders. He'd found home.

"Don't you dare put your arm around me and act like everything is all right." Suzie pushed his arm off and spun, glaring up at him. "I'm so mad at you. Get into the lodge so I can clean you up."

Grabbing his hand, she dragged him back inside. In the kitchen, she found a towel and dampened it under the tap. "What did you think you were doing?" she demanded as she dabbed gently at his bruised cheek. "There were two of them."

"I couldn't let them say those disgusting things about you." He thrust his jaw out stubbornly. "I'll never let that happen."

"Greyson, it's just words."

The way he looked at her, a lifetime of pain behind his gaze, it broke her heart. "I know how much *just words* hurt."

"But they said horrible things about you too."

"That's different."

"How?" *Did he not think he was worth standing up for?*

"It just is." He refused to meet her eyes.

Tenderly, she took his hand in hers, her fingers gently stroking his uninjured cheek as her heart broke again. *There must have been so much he'd been on the receiving end of over the years.* "I won't let anyone say anything about you either. Especially those good-for-nothing stepbrothers of yours. Good-for-nothing jealous jerks."

Finally, he lifted his haunted gaze to hers. Somehow it mingled with a tentative hope. "It's been a long time since anyone has stood up for me."

"You better get used to it. I defend what's mine."

"Am I yours?" The question hung there, fragile and earnest. Just like this complicated man in front of her.

Leaning forward, she brushed a featherlight kiss across his lips. "You're all I want for Christmas." It was the lightest of touches, and yet she was left breathless.

He pulled her into his arms. "I guess Christmas is coming a little early this year."

TWO DAYS TILL CHRISTMAS

The chair scraped along the floor as Hank leaned back in it, fixing an eye on Greyson. Fork raised half to his mouth, Greyson felt like a deer caught in the spotlight. "What?"

"It occurred to me that you are officially an employee of this ranch, and I reckon it's time we get you some clothes that reflect that."

He looked down at his threadbare clothes. "This will last a little longer."

"We can buy you some," Veronica said, resting her hand lightly on Hank's shoulder as she came to stand behind him.

The notion didn't sit well with Greyson. "It's generous of you, but I don't feel comfortable with that. I reckon I'll last until I can get a pay under my belt."

Veronica smiled gently at him. "How about we give you an advance on your first pay. It's not like you haven't been helping around the ranch."

Suzie held her forefinger up to halt any protests from him. "Just take the money. It's not a handout, it's an advance that you will earn."

Greyson rubbed the back of his neck. Maybe he was being a little silly. "I appreciate it."

Hank patted Veronica's hand. "If you don't need us this morning, reckon I'd better take him in before he can change his mind."

"I think that's a good idea." Veronica took her fiancé's dirty plate out of his hand. "It will be nice to not have you menfolk underfoot for a while. Us gals have some things to do as well." She flounced off to the sink.

Hank followed, wrapping his arms around her. Greyson pulled his gaze away from the loved-up couple and found Suzie watching him. "You should have seen them last year," she said.

"Bad?"

"No, but it took them a while to admit it to themselves. I was starting to think I'd have to shove them under the mistletoe myself to make it happen." She gave him a little wink. "Don't think I haven't thought about doing the same to you."

His heart beat faster as it always did whenever Suzie was so open about how she felt about him. He swallowed over his suddenly dry mouth. *Tell her.*

"Are you ready to head into town?"

Greyson wanted to throttle his new employer and his poor timing. He gave an apologetic smile to Suzie, hoping that she could somehow see in his eyes that there was more he wanted to say. "Reckon I am."

He reached out and gave her hand a squeeze. It was tame compared to the urge he had to take her into his arms and show her what the mistletoe really could do. Instead, he followed Hank to get their coats and head out to his truck.

The drive took place in that distinctly companionable silence that only cowboys had truly mastered. A few discussions on stock, football and maybe the weather, and then nothing. Even as the town appeared, the men maintained the easy quiet. Hank found a park and then, pulling his jacket a little tighter around him, braced himself for the cold outside. Greyson followed suit, except the wind's icy fingers went straight through his jacket.

"I need to head over to the bank first and get some money for you. If you want to go to Matherson's store, he stocks most of what you will be looking for."

Greyson nodded, grateful to be getting out of the cold. As the bells above the door jangled, he let the chill seep from his bones. Rows of clothing, boots and hats were neatly lined up, as well as various other paraphernalia. Self-consciously, he began to look at the clothes, turning the tags over to check prices. From the corner of his eye, he saw a display of brightly colored glass sculptures. One caught his eye. A brilliant confectionary of jewel tones that created a glorious gingerbread house.

"Is amazing, isn't it?" A man had quietly approached him while he'd been transfixed.

"It's ... I can't even wrap my head around the skill that went into making this." Greyson took in the detail. *Suzie would love this.* "Is it expensive?"

"Not as much as it should be. The artist is still unknown, and her pieces don't command as much they should. She's one to watch. She trained with Evelyn Hart, after all." The man thrust his chest out proudly. "The artist is my daughter."

Greyson took in the beaming father. "You have every right to be proud, she's talented. I know someone who would love to own it."

"Five hundred dollars is the best I can offer it to you. You can see the tag for yourself, it's marked at eight hundred."

Greyson's heart sank. He couldn't afford that even if it was a bargain. "I'm sorry, sir, I don't have the money."

"Don't have the money for what?" Hank asked as the jangling bells announced his arrival.

"It doesn't matter." Greyson thrust his hands dejectedly into his pockets.

"It doesn't look like it doesn't matter." Hank raised his brow at him. "It kinda looks like it matters a lot." He took out some cash and handed it over to Greyson. "Your advance."

Greyson stared down at it, surprised by the thickness. "How much of an advance did you give me?"

"Five hundred."

Somewhere, he was pretty sure angels started singing. "Excuse me, sir," Greyson chased after the shopkeeper who had walked away. "Do you sell little travel sewing kits?"

"Yes."

"I'll need one of those, and then I'll need you to wrap up that glass gingerbread house."

Hank looked puzzled. "What about clothes for you?"

Greyson grinned at him. "I've waited this long. They can last a little longer with mending. But I'm not leaving here without the perfect Christmas gift for Suzie. She's more important."

Hank quirked that brow at him again, amusement glinting in his eyes. "Reckon Suzie doesn't want you to freeze to death either."

"Trust me, thinking about her is more than enough to keep me warm."

Hank shook his head slowly, his lips stretching into a wry smile. "Boy, have you got it bad."

Greyson grinned back. "You have no idea."

THE SNOW SPRAYED in Suzie's face as she careened out of control down the slope, Lulu and Veronica on a sled beside her. She shrieked in childish delight as she went over a bump, almost getting dislodged from her plastic sled.

At last, she came to a stop and rolled of it onto her back. "Have I told you lately that I love the way you think?" she asked her friend. "When you said that us gals had some things to do, I was not anticipating this."

"Right back at you. I thought it was time for some fun. Without the men. So we can talk about the men." Veronica handed her sled to Lulu. "You go back up the hill. Suzie and I will wait for you down here." She watched as the girl trudged through the snow. "Ah, the energy of youth. I'm worn out." She flopped down beside Suzie. "So, let's talk about the men —or man. One in particular."

"Subtle." Suzie started making a snow angel.

"I thought so. It seems like things are going good with Greyson."

"I mean, I think so. It just feels a little like I made all the moves. But then, when his stepbrothers were here, he went all protective of my honor, which was kinda hot." Her stomach quivered at the maleness of him when he'd confronted his family.

"He's the double whammy of shy and low self-esteem combined with a country boy. I'm sure you'll have him whipped into shape in no time."

Suzie was still mulling her friend's words over later that night as she padded downstairs to get a glass of milk and saw the light shining out from underneath Greyson's bedroom door. *What was he doing still awake? Was he having trouble sleeping?* She knocked quietly.

"Come in."

She pushed open the door to find Greyson sitting underneath the lamp, a needle and thread in his hand as he mended some clothes. "This is the last thing I was expecting you to be doing."

He snipped the thread off between his teeth, holding the jeans up for inspection. Satisfied, he folded them neatly and put them to one side before picking up another article of clothing. "Waste not, want not."

Suzie suddenly remembered the package she had back in her room for him. "I have something I need to grab. I'll be right back." Once she'd returned, she looked down at her hands. *She didn't want him to feel like she was making fun of him.* She bit down on her lip as she handed it over. "Um, I got this for you. Actually, it's Lulu's idea. If you open it, I'll explain." She watched as he pulled the garish reindeer and glitter sweater from the bag. "Lulu wants us all to wear ugly sweaters on Christmas Eve. She helped pick everyone's. Except, instead of thinking they're ugly, she thinks they're amazing. Which, I guess if you look at them from a four-year old's eyes, they kinda are." She stopped when she saw the way he held it to his chest, his eyes shining. *Oh heck, she'd offended him.* "You don't have to wear it if you don't want to."

"I've never had an ugly sweater before." He looked at her, and her heart melted.

She took it from his hands and held it up. "And it's gloriously ugly."

"I think so." He let out a soft laugh under his breath as he took it back, hugging it to himself again. "Thank you."

"It was Lulu's idea." *Is it possible to be jealous of a sweater?*

"For letting me be a part of your Christmas." He looked down at the sweater again. "For not giving up on me. I know I don't gush and, well, I'm sure other guys have all the moves. I don't. Most the time, I don't even have the words." He gave a helpless shrug. "It doesn't mean that I don't care, I'm just learning how to show it."

Suzie's heart flip-flopped as he took a step closer, finally closing the distance between them. Her eyes darted about quickly. *Now would be an awesome time for some mistletoe.*

When none was forthcoming, her eyes were once again lost in his as he gently pushed a stray tendril of hair behind her ear. She'd washed it that night and hadn't styled it into its usual well-secured structure.

"Maybe you could help me learn."

"I'd like that," she whispered as his lips lowered to hers. "I'd like that a lot."

CHRISTMAS EVE

"*A*re those reindeer on your sweater actually pooping glitter?" Hank reached across the table for the green piping bag.

Greyson thrust his chest out proudly. "Yep."

"That's one heck of a sweater." Hank gave an experimental squeeze of the bag, causing it to let out a loud farting sound. "Oops."

"I'm not sure I've ever seen dachshunds pulling Santa's sleigh, especially not looking like they missed their rabies shot." Greyson added a pinch more sprinkles to his cookies. *You could never have too much sprinkle when a four-year-old was judging.*

"I think you'll find they're excited." Veronica added another cookie to the plate. "At least, that's what Lulu told me."

The little girl looked up from where she'd been very seriously adding ingredients into a large bowl. "Greyson?"

"Yeah, Lulu?"

"Is this ready?"

He carefully set his cookie beside the rest on the

snowflake patterned platter. Wiping his hands on his elf apron, he stepped closer to take a look at her handiwork. "I've never actually made reindeer food before, but I reckon it looks good enough to eat."

He made a show of reaching in to grab some. Squealing, she pulled the bowl safely out of reach. "It's not for you."

Greyson sighed. "Reindeer get all the good stuff."

"It's because they do all the important work for Santa," Lulu said with all the wisdom a four-year-old could muster.

"What about the elves?" Suzie asked. "Don't they do most of the important work? Like running his workshop."

"But the reindeer bring the presents to our house." Lulu was clearly willing to dig her heels in over this subject. "Santa can take some of the cookies home for the elves if he wants."

"That's generous of him," Hank muttered to his fiancé.

"Greyson?" Lulu tugged on his reindeer glitter poop festooned sleeve.

"Yeah?"

"You believe me, don't you?" She turned the full force of her little girl faith on him. "About the reindeer."

He scratched his chin as he made a show of mulling it over. "I'm a rancher, so I always think the stock are the most important things on a ranch. Don't see any reason why reindeer aren't the most important things at the North Pole."

Lulu beamed up at him before looking around him to poke her tongue out at the others. "See?" Her little hand crept into his. "You can help me put it out for them if you want."

"Hey, what about me?" Suzie protested. "I'm the one who showed you how to make it last year."

"That was last year," noted Hank. "This year, you're old news."

"If it makes you feel better, next year, Greyson will probably get passed over like we are now." Veronica gave him a sly look. "And then he'll be standing here with us."

Greyson chose to ignore the banter. He gestured for the girl to precede him. "This way, little lady. Those reindeer aren't going to feed themselves."

"Do you think that's how glitter is made?" Veronica asked as they trailed after them onto the porch.

"Don't be silly," Suzie said with a toss of her head. "Everyone knows unicorns make the best glitter."

It was a glorious night, a brightly shining star twinkling above as Lulu solemnly set her bowl down. The cold contrasted with the warmth of the house they'd just exited. Suzie blew on her hands. "If you're happy, Lulu, maybe we can get back inside."

"Before we all freeze to death, which wouldn't be very Christmassy at all," agreed Veronica.

Hank knelt down beside his daughter. "Are you happy with it, baby?"

Lulu wrapped her arm around her father's shoulders and leaned into him. Completely at ease in the love that surrounded her. "Last year, I made a wish and it came true. Do you think, if I made another one, it will again?"

"What wish did you make last year?" Hank asked.

"That you would kiss Veronica and she could be my mom." She stopped her little face scrunching up. "Is that two wishes?"

Greyson turned when he heard a little sob. Surprised, he saw both Suzie and Veronica dabbing at their eyes. "I'm pretty sure it counts as only one," Hank assured her.

"Can I tell you what I wish for this year?" Lulu glanced over her dad's shoulder to look at Greyson and Suzie.

Hank rocked a little on his heels to follow her gaze, a knowing smile gracing his lips. "I think maybe it's best you keep it to yourself. Just to be on the safe side. You can always tell me if it comes true."

Lulu settled back into her father. "I hope so, Dad."

Hank scooped his daughter into his arms and stood. "And now I think it's time we tuck you into bed."

"The sooner I go to bed, the sooner I'll wake up, and then it'll be Christmas." The little girl's eyes were shiny with excitement as she was carried inside.

"That's how I've been told it works," Hank said. Veronica followed her family up the stairs.

Suzie firmly took Greyson's hand in hers and led him to a spot right in front of the fire. "You stay here and warm up. I'm going to get us some eggnog."

Greyson settled onto the sofa, a wonderful warmth stealing over him. He wasn't sure how long he was staring into the flicker of the flames, mesmerized by the colors, before Suzie returned, handing a mug to him.

"My mom used to make eggnog by melting some vanilla ice-cream and putting whiskey in it." *Gosh he'd loved that stuff.* "Sometimes she'd get fancy and add some chocolate powder to the top." He stared down at his drink, complete with a candy cane sticking out of it. "I think I was a teenager before I found out that you didn't make it that way." It hit him that he would never be welcomed back at what had once been his family ranch. He would never show his children where he'd grown up or spend another Christmas there.

Suzie's hand crept into his again, somehow managing to convey a wealth of emotion in just a simple gesture. It was like her touch had direct access to his heart, a warm glow that flowed through him. "I think next year we should definitely add your mom's eggnog recipe to our Christmas traditions."

Greyson felt a sting in his eyes. "You would do that?"

"I don't know if you've noticed, but this is a pretty

patched-together family, and we wouldn't change it for the world. Maybe all this is a chance for a new beginning … with me." Suzie's eyes were serenely compelling.

It felt like she took his faded and careworn heart in her hands and repaired it with bright patches and love. "I'd like that." Heck, there were a lot of things he'd liked the sounds of lately. All of them involving Suzie.

She gave him an impish grin. "We seem to say that a lot to each other." Her eyes grew huge, and she bolted from the sofa. Heart pounding, Greyson wondered what he'd done to cause such a reaction. "Aha!" She crowed, triumphantly reaching into her stocking. "This is where I could ask if you want to play hide the pickle in my stocking." She brandished the green ornament about. "But I do believe I've found the pickle." She put her hands on her hips and, with a sassy wiggle of her hips, smirked at him. "Now, what is my prize?"

Now's your chance. Just say it. He moistened his mouth. Trying to put all his feelings into the way he looked at her, he opened his arms wide. "Me."

She flew into his arms. "And since it's what we say, I like the sound of that."

Greyson never did reply. She quite simply took the words from his mouth as she smothered him in kisses. Yep, he liked the sound of that too. Maybe Lulu's Christmas wish—or at least what he thought it was—might come true after all. The kid did seem to have a great strike rate.

CHRISTMAS DAY

*S*uzie wrinkled her nose in protest at the tinkling sensation. Opening her eyes, she gave a little squeal to find Lulu's face inches from hers. Wrapping her into a bear hug, she pulled her down. "Merry Christmas, Lulu. Has Santa been?"

"Yes, but you have to wake up first before we can start opening presents." Lulu gave her a reproachful glance. "You're the only one still in bed."

Suzie gave a satisfyingly bone-popping stretch. "I was keeping an eye out for reindeer last night."

She chuckled at Lulu's horrified expression. "You're not meant to do that, otherwise Santa won't come."

Suzie clucked the girl under the chin. "Well, good thing I went to bed. And you said there are presents, so Santa still came."

"Lucky. Now get up."

Suzie rolled over Lulu and bolted to the door. "Hurry up, Lulu, you can't stay in bed all day." Hearing the girl thrash about making her way off the bed, she hurried downstairs, flying on sock clad feet before coming to a rather undignified halt, Lulu bumping into her.

Veronica rolled her eyes at the spectacle, coming over to hand her a mug of cocoa. "Merry Christmas to you, too."

Suzie pulled her into a hug. "Merry Christmas." Over her friend's shoulder, she could see Greyson looking content as though he no longer had to keep himself rigidly self-contained. *Maybe Santa had sprinkled a little bit of Christmas magic. Good Lord knew Greyson deserved to feel accepted and appreciated.* "A certain Christmas elf woke me up to inform me that you were all waiting for me."

"Last year, you were the first to wake up," Hank noted dryly. "Did something—or someone—keep you up late on Christmas Eve?"

Suzie's gaze darted guiltily to the cause of her late night. "Just putting the mistletoe to good use."

Veronica snorted on her cup of cocoa. Greyson somehow managed to look both embarrassed and smug at the same time. *The man had talents.* Quite a few, as she was discovering.

Hank clapped his hands together. "Well, since everyone is here now, it's time to hand out the presents." He began to rifle through the gorgeously wrapped gifts under the tree. "Lulu. Another one for Lulu. Lulu." He paused, peering closer at a tag. "Lulu." He looked at his daughter in mock alarm. "I think Santa might have forgotten about everyone else."

"Don't be silly, Daddy. Santa wouldn't do that." Lulu giggled.

Veronica picked up a present. "Lulu." She added it to the growing pile. "Ah, Greyson." She smiled at him. "And here's one for Hank." In short order, the gifts had all been handed out.

Lulu had received everything from pink cowgirl boots to black tutus to a stuffed unicorn and a skateboard. *No one was ever going to be able to pigeonhole her.*

Suzie watched as Greyson opened his first present. He pulled back the paper to reveal a very expensive all-weather jacket and some jeans. A pair of keys fell out when he held the jacket up. "What's this?"

"We can't have our ranch hand driving a truck that isn't reliable." Hank put his arm around Veronica's shoulders.

"What?" Greyson stared at them incredulously.

"Go look out the window," Suzie said, having been in on the surprise. When they'd told her, she didn't think it would be possible to love her friends more. Greyson was staring outside before the words had even gotten out her mouth.

"Holy Kris Kringle. It's this year's model!" He spun back around to the room. "In black!" It appeared that he was having trouble breathing.

"Well, it is my favorite color," Suzie said.

"Thank you." Shock was still all over his face. "Thank you. I don't know what to say."

"I think you've more than said it," Veronica said.

"It doesn't seem enough." Greyson, a look passing over his face like he'd somehow come to a decision, made his way over to them. He wrapped his arm around Veronica and then Hank.

"Don't think just because we got you a truck that we're going to go easy on you," Hank blustered as he found himself pulled into a hug.

"Wouldn't have it any other way," Greyson said, his voice muffled.

"Here, open mine next. It isn't nearly as exciting," Suzie said, tickled pink at how happy Greyson was.

Slowly, he opened the box. A pair of new boots inside, a framed picture laying on top of them. He reached out a shaking finger. "Where'd you get that?"

"I found it in some old newspapers at the library in your

hometown." The picture was of his mother, onstage. "I remembered you saying that she liked to act."

Veronica peered over his shoulder. "She's beautiful."

"She was." Greyson blinked. "And the boots will keep my feet warm and dry." He gave a dry chuckle. "Been a while since I've been able to say that." He reverently placed the box to one side and got off the sofa. Reaching under the tree, he carefully extracted a box that had been hidden at the back. "I gave Hank instructions not to touch this one. I wasn't sure if my boss would listen." He teased Hank as he handed it over.

Suzie gently pulled back layers of tissue to reveal a delicate creation of colored glass. "My very own gingerbread house I can keep all year," she said in delight. The light reflecting off the sculpture had turned the inside of the box into a kaleidoscope. "It's beautiful."

"Can you see anything else?" pressed Greyson, his eyes intent.

She leaned in closer. On the chimney, a fragile chain had been wrapped, a shooting star pendant set with a diamond hanging from it. With shaking fingers, she tenderly unraveled it. "It's gorgeous."

"It was my mother's." Greyson came and took it from her fingers. "The only thing of value that Dad made sure I got of hers. I've carried it around with me for years. I never trusted leaving it in the house." He draped it around her neck. "When I first saw you all those years ago, you seemed just like this shooting star and just about as unattainable. Too far above someone like me. Now I realize how special it feels to be near you. My mother used to love fairytales and happy endings. And now, I think I do too." He stepped back around to be in front of her again. "Merry Christmas, Suzie."

Suzie's heart sang with pure Christmas delight as he cupped her chin and tenderly lifted her face to his. There was a heart-rendering tenderness to his kiss, one that promised words that were still to come. Maybe not today, but soon. And she quite liked the idea of that. Wrapping her arms firmly around her cowboy, she melted into him, ignoring Lulu's giggling and Hank covering his daughter's eyes. *After all, they were all family here.*

EPILOGUE

The tug on the necklace around Suzie's neck drew her loving gaze down to where the baby boy's fingers were twisted about the jewelry. Not once since the day her husband had put it there had she taken it off. Not through weddings—first theirs, and then their children's. First days of school. And now the arrival of their dearly cherished grandchild. The shooting star pendant had borne silent witness to it all, a life well lived, a wife well loved.

Tenderly, she untangled the infant's grip. Leaning closer to him, she breathed in his precious baby smell. Looking up, she smiled at the love of her life across the room standing beside Hank. All these years and children later, he and Veronica were still as much family as that very first Christmas. A smile ruffled the corners of Greyson's mouth. He was still a man of few words, but always managed to find the important ones.

"I love you," she mouthed.

Fine lines crinkled around his eyes. "I love you too," he soundlessly returned. Bending down, he reached under the Christmas tree. "Now, the first present is for Lulu."

SNEAK PEAK – LEVI (BOOK ONE OF THE BROTHERS OF CREEKSIDE RANCH SERIES)

"Here are your documents," the man Bella had known as Andrei—she still didn't know his real name—said before throwing them one at a time on the table in front of her. "Driver's license, birth certificate, social security number, passport."

Curiously, she picked them up. "Rebecca Callaghan." *Gosh she was tired.* "So, what does this Rebecca Callaghan do for a job?" She fingered the mousy brown wig they'd put her in. "Judging from how she looks, a dinner waitress?"

Andrei laughed. "It's good that you still have your sense of humor, especially after your long flight here. Tomorrow, you will have another short one and then you'll see where you're going to be staying."

Bella wanted to cry. When she'd first been approached by the FBI, it had seemed so noble. At least, that's what she'd told herself when she'd agreed to help them put Dmitri away. Deep in her soul, it had been to save herself. Each day, she'd felt that she was closer to him killing her in one of his games that he'd liked to play. Now the harsh reality was sinking in. She was far from home, looking like a drudge, and she didn't know when she'd be able to speak to her brother, let alone see him.

Biting her lip, she forced the tears away. Her parents hadn't raised her to have the famous British stiff upper lip for nothing. *I survived Dmitri, I can survive this.*

～

"Levi, I appreciate your assistance in this matter." Andrew, his old Navy SEAL buddy, extended his hand out. "You understand the need for discretion?"

"Sure thing." He took a seat opposite him. "You were pretty vague on the phone." It had come as a surprise to hear from him, especially asking for help with planting a rose bush. "I trust the rose is here?"

"She is. I can't tell you anything, you understand." Andrew held his gaze.

"Copy. The less I know the better." Levi cracked his knuckles. "The timing works out well."

"I thought so." Andrew scratched at the back of his neck. "I guess it's time you meet her."

Curiously, he followed Andrew into the other room and stopped, eyeing the delicate beauty in front of him. The horrendous mousey brown wig did little to hide the delicate English rose complexion, nor the large albeit exhausted eyes, rimmed as they were in shadows of fatigue. Levi turned to his friend. "I don't think this is going to work. She's not cut out for where she's going."

"Excuse me?" the woman said in a posh British accent. "I think you'll find you'll quit before I do."

"Sweetheart, I'm a Navy SEAL. Quitting ain't in my vocabulary." He leaned closer to glower at her.

"I'm—" She stopped. Recovering, she glared down her

pert little nose at him. "Well, if I could tell you what I am, you'd be shaking in your boots before your betters."

"Good to see you two getting on."

"Who is this loathsome man?"

Andrew hid his smile when Levi glowered at him. "Rebecca, this is Levi. Levi, this is Rebecca. Rebecca, you are going to be the nanny to his little sister on their family ranch."

"Which means, sweetheart, I'm your boss."

"Like heck it does." Alarmed, she glanced toward Andrew in appeal. "Surely there are other, better, more suitable options."

"Unfortunately for you and me both, I'm it." Levi liked the way she bit down hard on her bottom lip as she thrust her stubborn little chin out. "So, Beccy, you better start liking the idea." Good Lord knew he was starting to.

Levi available on Amazon and in Kindle Unlimited here

ACKNOWLEDGMENTS

A debt of gratitude to my editor Rebekah Groves for her patience with me.

Another big thanks to Megan from Designed with Grace for her cover design.

To my amazing beta readers and street team, you guys rock and I couldn't do it without you.

And finally to my fabulous alpha reader Trixie Norman, for all the late nights of reading and endless questions about your thoughts.

ALSO BY EDITH MACKENZIE

Have you read them all?

Cowboy Christmas Series

The Mistletoe Collection

Boots and Mistletoe

Cowboy boots, mistletoe, and a holiday do-over…

Buy Now

The Cowboy Under the Mistletoe

It'll take more than the magic of the season to help this grump find her happily ever after…

Buy Now

Mistletoe and the Billionaire's Cowgirl

He's the last man she wants this holiday season. Too bad he's exactly what she needs…

Buy Now

The Christmas Star Collection

The Cowboy's Christmas Star

Can the starlet lasso her cowboy in time for Christmas carols and mistletoe?

Buy Now

Her Reluctant Cowboy Christmas Star

Romance isn't for the weak. Good thing he's tougher than he *thinks* he is…

Buy Now

Billionaire Hearts Ranch Series

The wounded cowboy billionaire

He had all the money in the world—and it wasn't enough to keep his life from falling apart…

Buy Now

The billionairess' cowboy

He broke her heart once. She's not about to let him do it again…

Buy Now

The billionaire's cowgirl

They were polar opposites who thought they had it all…until they met each other…

Buy Now

The cowgirl's fake billionaire marriage

There's one rule in their fake marriage--don't fall in love. But rules are meant to be broken...right?

Buy Now

A cowboy's riches (Prequel)

She's broken free and is ready to fly…or ride, as the case may be…

Buy Now

Billionaires Lonely Hearts Club

Red Dust and The Billionaire

Wild horses couldn't drag this couple to happily ever after…right?

Buy Now

Star Dust and The Billionaire

It'll take more than star dust and Hollywood magic to get *this* couple to happily ever after…

Buy Now

Gold Dust and The Billionaire

His friends can settle down, but *he* won't. Or so he kept telling himself…

Buy Now

The Brothers of Creekside Ranch Series

Levi

Levi and Bella's story

Pre Order Now

Amos

Pre Order Now

Elijah

Pre Order Now

Barrels and Hearts series

Available on Amazon and Kindle Unlimited

A Bull Rider's Paradise

The prequel to the Barrels and Hearts series. True love is only the beginning….of the story. Find out where it all began with Ana and Eduardo. Sometimes finding love is easy. It's keeping it that's hard.

Buy here

A Cowgirl's Dream

An Aussie cowgirl far from home. A handsome Brazilian bull rider. Can they have a rodeo love story of their dreams?

Buy Now

A Cowgirl's Heart

An Aussie cowgirl in need. Her childhood friend to the rescue. Can friendship turn into a love story?

Buy Now

A Cowgirl's Passion

One feisty cowgirl. One steadfast Brazilian bull rider. Will she see what is right in front of her?

Buy Now

A Cowgirl's Pride

An Aussie cowgirl from the wrong side of the tracks. A handsome equine vet. Can they find a way to have their happy ever after?

Buy Now

A Cowgirl's Love

A young Aussie cowgirl. A widowed rancher. Does age matter when it comes to love?

Buy Now

A Cowgirl's Movie Star

A fiery cowgirl with big dreams. A movie star far from home. When their two worlds collide, will their love be strong enough to hold them together or will they be pulled apart

Buy Now

A Cowgirl's Billionaire

A cowgirl adrift. A broken billionaire cowboy. Can he free himself from the past to be the man she needs now?

Buy Now

Cowboy Christmas Series

The Mistletoe Collection

Boots and Mistletoe

Cowboy boots, mistletoe, and a holiday do-over…

Buy Now

The Cowboy Under the Mistletoe

It'll take more than the magic of the season to help this grump find her happily ever after…

Buy Now

Mistletoe and the Billionaire's Cowgirl

He's the last man she wants this holiday season. Too bad he's exactly what she needs…

Buy Now

ABOUT THE AUTHOR

Edith MacKenzie or Eddie Mac to her friends is an author of sweet and wholesome contemporary cowboy romance. They say in literary circles to write what you know, and Eddie has certainly taken that to heart. Before embarking on a writing career, she trained horses professionally and brings that wealth of knowledge to her writing.

Now a mum to a boy and girl, as well as wife, she delights with her tales of strong cowgirls and their adventures in finding love. When not weaving the love stories of her characters, she enjoys hanging out with her family and animals, as well as reading, fishing and camping.

Just remember—once a cowgirl, always a cowgirl.

facebook.com/EddieMacAuthor
instagram.com/edith_mackenzie_author
amazon.com/Edith-MacKenzie
bookbub.com/profile/edith-mackenzie
twitter.com/edith_mackenzie